FINN AND HIS COMPANIONS

ST PATRICK WELCOMES HIS GUESTS.

FINN
AND HIS COMPANIONS

BY
STANDISH O'GRADY

AUTHOR OF
"THE FLIGHT OF THE EAGLE," ETC.

Fredonia Books
Amsterdam, The Netherlands

Finn and His Companions

by
Standish O'Grady

ISBN: 1-4101-0208-4

Fredonia Books
Amsterdam, The Netherlands
http://www.fredoniabooks.com

PREFACE

You have, I am sure, often heard how the Roman Empire was broken up and destroyed by the barbarians of Northern Europe, the Goths, the Vandals, the Huns, the Picts, and Scots, etc., etc. You know too, why God permitted this to be done. It was because the civilised Romans, and the nations whom they made like themselves, lost the great simple virtues of truth, courage, generosity, and the readiness to sacrifice their lives and possessions for the sake of noble objects. We read that Romans at this time would even cut off their thumbs in order to avoid becoming soldiers; for, of course, a young man who had no thumb to his hand could not be expected to hold a spear strongly, or wield a sword well. In those days the rich Roman became not only very rich, but also selfish and ease-loving, and the poor Roman very poor, so that he cared about nothing but how he might get food in order that he might live; and generally the Roman character changed greatly from what it was in ancient times, for wealth, commerce, civilisation, and peace, however good in themselves, have this tendency, viz. they enfeeble and corrupt men's minds, and make them selfish, lazy, and hard-hearted. Then, as God long ago sent the flood to drown a world which had grown too wicked, so he sent the brave though rude barbarians of northern Europe to destroy the Romans and break their great Empire to pieces.

> Woe to the lands, the minstrel sang,
> That hear the northern warriors' clang.

You have also read in the English histories how at this time the Romanised Britons were perpetually invaded and plundered by the Picts and Scots, and then by the Saxons, until they were quite ruined. The Picts and Scots and the Saxons could not have done this in the time of Caractacus and Boadicea.

Now it becomes an interesting question what kind of men these northern barbarians were who did such a great work, and one would like to know how they lived, what they loved and honoured, and what they hated and despised. Of the other northern nations other writers will tell you something. I am going to tell you something about the nation which in histories of England are called the Scots. Now the Scots, who, in alliance with the Picts made such havoc among the degenerate Britons, were in fact the Irish, who at some very early period, overflowing out of Ireland, occupied the western counties of Scotland. The Highlanders and the Irish of Ireland were one race of people whom the old historians called *Scoti* or Scots. They spoke the same language, and had the same manners and customs, and the same traditions, the same music and the same songs. A great many of their songs and stories lingered a long time in the Highlands, and

were believed to have been made by a poet called
Ossian. In Ireland a still greater number remained
in the minds of the people. These songs and stories,
too, were attributed to Ossian or to friends of
Ossian, and have been from time to time written
down on paper or on parchment. In these stories
we learn a great deal about Ossian, his friends and
acquaintances, what sort of men they were, and how
they lived. I do not say that everything related
about them is true, but when we compare these
stories with what is known historically about the
conquerors of the Roman Empire, we can see that
the people amongst whom Ossian lived must have
been very like the people of the Ossianic stories, and
that Finn, who was the father of Ossian, Oscur his
son, Diarmid his chivalrous cousin, Caelta, Mac-
Lewy, and the rest were very brave, upright, true-
hearted, and affectionate men, who in their forests
and their rude simple homes preserved certain
virtues which the Romans and the Romanised
Britons had lost in spite of all their wealth. These
stories will, I hope, amuse and entertain you, and
will also enable you to read some meaning in a word
which you have often seen in your histories, but
which has had hitherto for you no meaning at all,
or perhaps a bad one. The Scots, who with the
Picts gave the poor degenerate Britons so many
beatings in battle and plundered them far and wide,
were essentially somewhat like the men whose
characters and manner of living you will find
described in these stories. Most of our stories

relating to this period are supposed to have been told by Ossian to St. Patrick. Those which I relate are, for the most part, stories told to St. Patrick by Caelta, a cousin of Ossian, and are not so well known. Most of them are, I think, quite new. If all our Irish Ossianic stories and poems were published, I daresay they would fill a hundred volumes like the present. I have, however, tried to tell these few stories in such a way as to give you a good general idea of the literature as a whole.

Finn and his friends are believed to have flourished in the second and third centuries, that is about two hundred years before the Irish began to break out and attack the Roman Empire in this part of Europe.

The great influence exercised by Finn over the Irish mind was not destroyed, but rather purified and elevated, by the introduction of Christianity. It is distinctly traceable down to the seventeenth century, and though now unrecognised, perhaps still survives, warring strongly, if silently, against the vices which are always connected with civilisation.

CONTENTS

CONTENTS

PART III

FINN AND THE HISTORIAN

PART IV.

THE COMING OF FINN

PART I

SAINT AND HERO

Long, long ago, beyond the misty space
  Of twice a thousand years,
In Erin old there lived a mighty race,
  Taller than Roman spears.

Finn and His Companions

CHAPTER I.

ST. PATRICK AND HIS STRANGE GUESTS.

ST. PATRICK and his fellow-missionaries were building a little church made of straight trees interlaced with osiers on the plains of Meath at a place near the river Boyne, westward from Tara. The sun was declining, and the pious Britons worked industriously, making the most of what daylight still remained. A young clerk who was laying the timbers of the roof cried out, "Look, brothers! What great men are these who come towards us with large strides? Sad yet noble are their faces. Truly, I have not seen such in this land at any time." So he stood looking, with a plank in one hand and a hammer in the other.

St. Patrick looked towards Tara and saw ten men coming towards him and now very near. The tallest of the tonsured Gaels and Britons who were with Patrick would

not reach their shoulder-blades, and hardly
to the waist of the man who walked before
the others and seemed to be their captain.
They wore shields and swords, and in their
hands carried spears proportioned to their
size and strength. Each man's mantle,
blue, green, or scarlet, was folded round his
shoulders and fastened on the breast by
brooches the rings of which were like wheels
of gold or silver. Their knees were bare,
and their hair, escaped from the brazen
helmets, fell in dense curling masses on
their shoulders. Their port was majestic,
and the meanest of them carried himself
like a king. Nevertheless, as the young
clerk had said, their countenances were sad,
as of men who lacked their comrades, or had
recently lost their dear lord.

St. Patrick in his white garments, and
bearing his bent staff in his hand, went to
meet them, and gave them a respectful and
affectionate greeting and bade them a welcome to his small monastery. He conducted
them himself to the guest-house. His people
brought lavers and washed their feet and
hands. They were struck with great awe
as they observed the nobleness of the men,
their mighty limbs, their tranquillity, and

their silence. Food fit for kings was set before them, and old ale in handsome vessels. There, sitting on couches, they ate and drank a little and said nothing, and St. Patrick ministered to them with his own hands, and the more he looked upon them the more he loved them. When all had been served, St. Patrick himself sat down upon a couch over against their captain, and as he did so the men stood up and made him a reverence and again sat down. Though the young men of the monastery frequently made the circuit of the chamber to pour out ale, they soon found that the men's cups continued full. At a sign from St. Patrick they withdrew; nevertheless the silence was not broken.

The Pagan then raised his eyes and contemplated the Christian for a long time. He knew well the faces of druids, but such a druid as this he had never seen before, and he marvelled at the goodness, refinement, and purity which shone in every feature. St. Patrick on the other hand contemplated the Pagan, his large, bright, peerless eyes and the simplicity and majesty of his aspect, and the more he looked the more he marvelled.

CHAPTER II.

ST. PATRICK CONVERSES WITH THE GREAT MEN.

THEN the Saint became aware that the expression of his guest's countenance altered to one of sharp inquiry, and, as if answering his thoughts, he said,

" What wouldst thou, O warrior?"

" Tidings of my dear foster-brother Ossian, O holy druid on whose head has come the razor."

Ere the Saint could reply a young and very handsome clerk who sat near him started up, smote his hands together, and, signing the air with the symbol of the cross, cried aloud in the Latin tongue, " God and His holy angels protect us. My father, this is a dead man. *Occisus est in prælio Gabran*" (he was slain in the battle of Gabhra) " in the reign of Cairbré of the Liffey, son of Cormac mac Art. These men are apparitions, or they are the *Sidhe* (the Shee)."

The youth was Benignus. He was a Gael, and learned in his country's history What he called " the Shee" were the gods

of the Pagan Irish. At the name of
" Gabhra" the men bowed their heads, and
their captain put his great hands over his
face and wept silently. After a while
Patrick said—

" Of thy dear foster-brother Ossian I
have no tidings. But who art thou, O noble
man, and who are these with thee? I ask
that I may be the better able to serve thee."

A torrent of loving-kindness and compassion poured from the saint's heart
towards him as he spoke. Also he endeav-
oured to calm the agitation of his young
friend and disciple Benignus, who said they
were dead men or gods.

" I am Caelta the son of Ronan,"
answered the large man. " We are all that
remain in the whole world of Finn's heroes,
unless, mayhap, magnanimous Ossian, his
incomparable son, be still alive in some isle
of the sea beyond the setting of the sun.
Thy druidic community, I perceive, are
strangers in Erin. Is the King of Erin kind
to thee, who art thyself kind to strangers?
Say he is not, O Talkend,* and verily he
shall be compelled."

* Talkend means ' razored head,' an allusion to the
saint's tonsure.

"Nay," answered Patrick, "Laeghaire, son of Nial, hath been very kind to us."

"Who is that man?" said Caelta, more sternly. "Are thy spells upon us, O druid, for that man is not in Ireland?"

His voice in its rising wrath was terrible to hear and shook the guest-house.

"I am no druid," answered Patrick mildly, "and have no understanding of spells, charms, and incantations. Truly, Laeghaire, son of Nial of the Nine Hostages, is now King of Ireland, whoever was King in thy time. Benignus, tell these noble men the pedigree of the King, and how he stands related in descent or otherwise with him who reigned when the battle of Gabhra was fought."

Benignus thereupon spoke out very clearly and fluently, for sweet was his voice, and eloquent was the young man. It was he who used to chant hymns and canticles for Patrick, and revive his spirits when they drooped.

"Noble strangers," he said, "the King of Ireland now is indeed Laeghaire, son of Nial of the Nine Hostages, who was the son of Eocha Moymodhon, who was the son of Murdach, who was the son of Fiacha, who was the son of Cairbré of the Liffey. And in the reign of Cairbré of the Liffey was fought the great battle of Gabhra, where were exterminated the giant race of the Fians, falling by each other's hands in fratricidal warfare, so that only nine men went alive out of the battle around Caelta son of Ronan, and from that day to this they have not been seen. Also there survived Ossian the son of Finn, but he was not in the battle, for he went out of Ireland before that, and there are no tidings of him since he followed the Danann maiden beyond the setting of the sun." The men looked at each other in great amazement.

" Where have you been since the battle ?" asked Patrick.

" We went out of the battle," said Caelta, " after having raised the tombs of our dead, and after having mourned long, weeping passionately, over the grave of Oscur, to the house of the prophetess and wisest of all women, Kama, who had cared for and watched over Finn since he was a boy. And she asked tidings of the Fians and why we came to her so few, so sad, and so torn with many wounds, and when we told her she raised up her voice and wept aloud. Then we all wept together, lamenting as it were the end of the world, on account of the great destruction that had come upon the Fians. After that she washed our wounds and bound them up, applying salves and ointments and incantations of power, and gave us the newest of food and the oldest of drink, and sweetly we slept that night in her enchanted house, and our great sorrow departed; and ever delicious fairy music resounded under the hollow dome, so that it was sweeter to be awake there than to sleep. Nevertheless she would not suffer us to go beyond her doors, nor were we ourselves inclined to do so on account of the lassitude and weakness which had come upon us after the battle; yet we felt no pain or grief, and that indeed surprised us, for it is not usual with good men whose dear friends have been slain to feel such peace of mind as we experienced in the house of the prophetess. Four days and nights we were with her, and on the morning of the fifth I said to my men, ' It is time for us to go. Why should we be burthensome to kind hosts? Let us go elsewhere if there are yet in Erin those who will be kind to us on account of our kindness to them in the day of our power.'

"When we came to bid the woman fare-well, she wept anew a long time, and she said that we would not meet again any more till the day of the final harmonising of all the world's discordant things. And she directed us to come first to this place, where holy druids would be kind to us and instruct us. Verily, O Talkend, our parting from the woman was like the parting of body and soul, and when we put our feet outside her fairy threshold and saw the green grass and the resplendent sun, full remembrance came upon us again, and great sorrow and weep-ing, so that with one accord we drew back our feet. But when we thought to recross the threshold, the house which we had left was not seen, nor the woman. There was nothing there save the green hillside and a murmuring stream. Then having wept again, we did as the woman directed, and came to this place. Truly we were under spells in that palace, and our days there were the generations of men."

CHAPTER III.

ANGELS INSTRUCT ST. PATRICK AS TO FINN.

PATRICK rejoiced greatly when he heard these words, for he perceived that the men had been miraculously preserved by the power of the Almighty, that he, Patrick, might teach them the true faith, and that they might be baptized by his hands, and he shed tears of joy for that reason, and on account of his ardent affection for the men. Then he arose and kissed the ten men one after another and blessed them, beginning with Caelta, and again sat down, and drew his white raiment over his face and wept. Then all wept together, the Saint for pure joy and the heroes for pure sorrow on account of the strange things and men amongst whom they had drifted in the tide of time.

After that Patrick asked Caelta many questions concerning Finn and the Fians and concerning their thoughts and manner of life, and Caelta answered all well, for he was rarely intelligent, and moreover he possessed the gift of eloquence, and Patrick

rejoiced listening to him. When their conversation had lasted a good while, Patrick
said—

" How came you, the Fians, to have such
power, when the knowledge of the true God
was denied to you ?"

And Caelta answered—

" O Talkend, it was because we had
truth in our hearts, strength in our hands,
and discretion in our tongues."

Patrick called a young man who was his
scribe to take his tablets and write down
that speech of the Fian's.

He also asked him what manner of man
was Finn.

And Caelta said : " There has not come
upon the earth a man like him since the beginning of the world nor will till the end of
time. That, O Talkend, is, in a little, what
I have to say concerning Finn. But if I
were to pronounce his complete eulogy, the
morning with its full light would not find
me near the end."

And of Ossian he said, not that he was
a famous poet, but that he was a famous
warrior, and renowned above all the rest for
magnanimity and liberality. " Ossian," he
said, " never asked anything from any man,

and never refused any man anything. For himself he was willing to keep only the head with which he ate and the feet with which he walked."

" That is a great character," said St Patrick, and he bade Bricna, the scribe, write it down. " It is not greater than the man to whom I attribute it," said Caelta.

Next day St. Patrick arose while it was still dark, and walked meditating along the banks of the slow-moving royal Boyne, between the trees and the river, revolving many things. As at other times, angels of God met him, and he asked them whether it was displeasing to God that he should feel so much delight in the profane conversation of the great Pagans. And the angels said that it was not, but pleasing, and that Finn, though a Gentile, was nevertheless a prophet without full knowledge, and had prepared the minds of the Gael for the preaching of Christ's gospel, and they also bade him write in a book such things as Caelta might tell him, for the instruction of future generations. " For truly," they said, " the Holy Trinity have been in this place before thee."

After that the angels left him and

St. Patrick returned to the monastery with
great joy. The men were still asleep. They
slept two days and three nights before the
Saint conversed with them again.

Patrick baptized them, and after they
had been baptized Caelta put his hand into
the hollow of his mighty shield and took out
a bar of gold and gave it to Patrick as his
baptismal fee. It was as thick as a man's
arm and reached from the elbow of the
Saint to the first joint of his forefinger.

" It came from a good man," said Caelta,
" and it goes to another. This was the last
payment that I had from my dear lord and
friend, Finn the son of Cool, the son of
Trenmor, high captain of the Fianna of
Erin."

From that bar Patrick made gilding for
all his bells and books, and rejoiced to think
that his sacred things had their gold from
such a source, for the conversation of Caelta
and the communications of the angels
caused him to perceive that Finn was a seer
and a prophet who in his own way, not
knowing it, wrought out the will of God
amongst the Gael. Also he was careful to
record all that Caelta related to him concerning Finn and the Fians.

PART II

FINN AND THE CURMUDGEON

CHAPTER I.

FINN GOES A-HUNTING.

FINN and his men went on a hunting expedition to one of his great forests in Leinster, for the Fians had forests in all parts of Ireland, and no one dared to hunt in them or kill any game there without Finn's permission. Early in the morning, before the sun had yet risen, they entered the forest. Each huntsman held back a straining hound by a leash which passed through a ring in the hound's collar. He held in his hands the two ends of the leash; when he wished to let the hound slip, he loosed one of the ends of the leash. Before them went the beaters with long sticks, beating the brakes and coppices and rousing the game. Between the places that gave cover for the game there was much open and smooth ground. Finn himself was on the right of the line of huntsmen, leading his favourite hound Bran.

The first animal that they started was a wild boar. He could not be seen from the

place where Finn stood, but the sound of the
horn on the left gave notice that some great
game had been roused, and the cries of the
hunters and the loud baying of the hounds
showed that it was some great beast. " That
is a boar," said Finn to the hunter who was
next to him.   " He is charging down our
way and killing or maiming every dog
which is loosed upon him." Presently the
boar broke through a coppice; his eyes were
like fire and his white tusks red with blood;
the bristles on his neck stood up like rods,
and the froth flew from his mouth like snow.
Some of the huntsmen refused to slip their
hounds against such a beast.   Three were
loosed upon him after he passed the coppice; one he tossed over his head, and the
second he trampled and maimed, the third
only stood at a distance and howled. Then
Finn slipped Bran.   So swiftly flew Bran
upon the boar that her track was like a black
and yellow flash over the green turf, and at
her baying as she was let loose the hollows
of the distant mountains rang, and far away
husbandmen labouring in fields said,
" Hark! that is the voice of Bran. The
Fians are abroad to-day; they have let loose
Bran."   Bran seized the huge boar by the

throat and shook him to and fro as a puppy-
dog shakes a rag.

Then leaving the boar dead, she returned
to be caressed and made much of by her
master, who said, "My brave Bran, thou
hast not done such a deed since the son of
the great enchanter Angus Ogue, having
taken a boar's form, was dragged down by
thee."

So while the red sun climbed the sky,
Finn's men advanced through the forest.
The horns continually sounded, and the
mingled baying of the hounds, and the cries
of the hunters cheering on their dogs, made
a sweet music. Many of the poor people of
the country, who dwelt in the borders of
that forest, stood on the neighbouring hills
and watched the scene with great joy.
Before noon there were killed many boars
and badgers, many an antlered stag, many
wolves, and as for hares and such like small
game, it would have been hard to count
them.   So eager were the huntsmen that
they did not feel hunger till the sun was
nigh his setting.

CHAPTER II.

FINN LOOKING FOR HOSPITALITY MEETS
A CURMUDGEON.

THEN said Finn to some of his people who
knew that country—

" Is there any lord or wealthy *bru-fear*
living hard by, who can give us good entertainment to-night?"

They said, " There is not."

" I marvel how you can say that," said
Finn, " for it is but little time since I myself saw the mansion of such a one. It is in
a green and fertile valley beyond the forest
in the west, large and handsome, and the
walls white with lime. I saw an orchard
gay with apple-blossom and stacked corn
and all the outward signs of good living."

Thereat they laughed and said—

" We shall get no entertainment there,
O Captain of the Fianna of Erin. The
owner of that house is the least hospitable
man in Ireland. Many a stranger has gone
thither and departed as he came."

Finn was very angry, and said—

" I swear by the generous and all-liberal

Sun who has ripened that churl's corn and given him wealth and abundance, that he shall yield hospitality to me and the Fians this night with his will or against it."

Then calling to him a trusty attendant, he said—

"O Dering, go to that man and say that Finn, the son of Cool, Captain of the Fianna Eireann, requests entertainment and rest for his people now spent with the chase and famished with sharp hunger."

So saying, Finn winded his horn to summon to him his scattered men.

Dering having gone, returned, and standing before Finn, said—

"O Captain of the Fianna, I went to the man according to thy command. He was sitting at the end of his table with his people about him at supper, which I perceived to be a very meagre repast. His wife sat at his right hand, her look was as kind and gentle as his was not, and she is very beautiful. I walked up the hall to where he sat, and having made a fitting reverence delivered thy message in thy very words. Yet he answered sternly, ' Go back and tell thy master that he and his young men may roast their own supper in Fian ovens as they

are accustomed to do, and couch themselves
in thick brakes, for they are healthy and
hardy. From me he will get no entertainment.'"

Before he had made an end of speaking
Finn strode in anger through the forest in
the direction of the man's house. Finn
entered the inhospitable house, where the
master had just risen from supper; he
seized him with his left hand and threw him
on his knees, and while he was in that
posture addressed him thus—

"As thou hast not given hospitality to
us willingly thou shalt give it unwillingly.
From the rafters of thy house, hanging
there with a rope round thy breast, thou
shalt this night look down uncomfortably on
the consumption of thy goods. Then I think
thy covetous soul will be much distressed;
and mark this, too, that when I leave in the
morning the cord will not be around thy
breast, that all men may know how loath-
some are covetousness and inhospitality in
my eyes."

A long cord was then procured, and
when a running loop had been made in it at
one end and the hands of the man tied
together, it was put round his breast under

the arm-pits. In the centre of the house
there was a tall smooth tree which was the
main support of the roof and therefore was
called the roof-tree. One of Finn's grandsons, holding the end of the cord in
his teeth, swarmed up the roof-tree, and,
passing the cord over one of the cross
beams, slid down again, bringing the
cord with him. Then they hoisted the
curmudgeon and drew him swiftly up till
his poll struck against the cross beam and
they wound the cord round the roof-tree and
made it fast. There, pale and astonished,
the owner of the house looked down upon
the scene while Finn issued his orders to the
house-steward and to the servants.

CHAPTER III.

THE CURMUDGEON SAVED BY HIS WIFE.

THE chamber in which these things were
done was the great central hall of the
palace. At the end of this hall, facing the
door of the house, there was a small door
having carved jambs and a carved lintel,
which communicated with inner chambers—

the quarters which were reserved for women
only. Hardly had Finn's people made fast
the cord round the foot of the roof-tree when
from these inner chambers there arose loud
cries and lamentations. Presently the door
was opened and a young woman beautifully
attired stood in the doorway. She was very
fair and shone like a star against the dark
background. It was the man's wife. Anyone looking at him would have supposed
that the curmudgeon was made fast in the
cord of his slaughter; but a full account of
what had been done was brought to the
woman, and she knew that her husband was
more frightened than hurt. For a moment
she stood still, while her eyes travelled
round the great chamber filled with strange
forms of men, then letting fall her veil she
hastened down, followed by her attendants,
who wept and smote their hands together,
and cast herself before Finn's feet weeping.

Finn was moved by her beauty and her
distress, and said : " Name thy petition, my
child, for it is already granted."

And she said—

" O Captain of the Fians, spare my husband, and I promise from him and from
myself that all thy people shall be well and

liberally entertained, as is only right.   I
looked for no other end of our slender house-
keeping, and lo, I have beside me much store
of food and drink reserved for some such
day of destruction as hath now come upon
us."

And Finn said : " O Lady, I perceive
that thou art wise as well as fair.   Thy
boon is granted, and by my right hand I
swear that had I known this man was dear
to thee, though greatly angered, I would not
have put him to such shame."

CHAPTER IV.

GOOD CHEER IN THE HOUSE OF INHOSPITALITY.

THEN the curmudgeon was let down from
his uncomfortable position and untied, and
Finn and his men left the house and went in
quest of the remainder of the Fians.   The
latter had in the meantime come together
from different parts of the great forest to
the place where Finn had winded his horn,
and when they did not find him there their
trackers traced him till they came to a place
which commanded a distant view of that
green valley in which was the great white

inhospitable house, and lo, from all the chimneys of the same there went up thick rolling pillars of dark smoke to the violet sky, each distinct and straight, for it was a windless evening.   When the Fianna saw that sight their laughter was loud and long, yea, though they were sore spent with the chase they laughed till their tears flowed and they leaned against each other for laughing, and one said to another, " It is easy to see that Finn has paid an early visit to that house."   And also, " The man who is called Nod must get to himself another name from this night," for in their language the name Nod meant " stinginess."

Then they met Finn, and afterwards all went together to an adjoining lake and bathed there, and the surrounding woods and hills resounded with their cries and joyful exclamations and laughter as they swam to and fro there like waterfowl and beat the still lake into foaming waves as if a hurricane had descended upon its quiet surface.   There was always a lake or river in the neighbourhood of Finn's forests, and when there was not he commanded a lake to be dug.   When they came out of the lake their attendants handed to each of them a

change of raiment, bright banqueting
attire, and after that they all proceeded
together joyfully to "the house of inhospitality."

Now, though Finn and his companions
had often been well entertained in many
houses, they agreed that they had seldom
been so well entertained as they were that
night. For, not only was the fare good and
abundant, and the drink likewise, but the
banqueting table flashed throughout from
end to end with vessels of silver and gold,
and cups of dazzling crystal, and the table
linen was of the finest texture and inlaid
with curious patterns, for by the advice of
his prudent wife the man Nod brought forth
all his hidden treasures and jewels of great
price, which he had amassed and had stored
away in dark places. Moreover, the man
and his wife—the man impelled by fear and
the woman by her own generous heart—
exerted themselves to the utmost in order
that every desire of their strange guests
might be satisfied. The attendants and the
dog-boys and the dogs, the tired beaters, too,
were all royally entertained, each according
to his degree. Cheerful was the laughter
of the heroes in the inhospitable house, and

their hearts rejoiced greatly to think that
in such a house these things could be. After
supper was ended Finn called for music, and
his harpers harped before him, and also
Ossian, the son of Finn, chaunted for them
a tale of some ancient woe, and bowed all
their heads and relaxed their hearts. After
that they sang Fian songs full-toned and
strong, singing loud all together with open
mouths, songs of war or of the chase or of
adventure, rejoicing in their glory and their
matchless career, and far away the Leinster-
men heard them, both those who dwelt by the
eastern sea and those who lived along the
green borders of the Barrow, for it was not
a little noise that Finn's men made when
they sang. So the Fians passed that evening in the house of inhospitality, and those
of Nod's people who witnessed the scene
used to speak about it as long as they lived.
When it grew towards the hour for sleep
Finn called for his little magic tympan or
lyre, of which long since he had mightily
deprived Allen, the son of Midna the
enchanter, and he gently touched the
strings. The virtue of this lyre was such
that no man could hear it without sleeping
well afterwards. When Finn played on

this lyre it was a signal to his men that they should go to rest. This night each hero found a good bed ready to receive him and all of less degree also, according to what was customary in houses of hospitality or even better, and the hounds too, such as the great boar had not slain, were abundantly provided with clean straw. There Finn and all his people slept sweetly, but the man Nod and his wife took counsel together, and made preparations so that in the morning their guests might break their fast well.

They all breakfasted next morning in the gloaming, and departed with the rising of the sun. Finn saluted the lady respectfully and afterwards her lord cheerfully, only he added with a stern look, " Come to me to the Hill of Allen on the tenth day." So Finn and his people and their numerous dogs passed away, and the noisy and many-coloured procession entered the woods, going swiftly, so that soon even the sound of their voices was not heard and a great silence reigned over the whole valley. Nod and his wife were standing together at the door of the mansion, and they turned and looked at each other without speech.

Nod's substance was not impaired by

that extensive billeting of Finn's men and hounds, such was the amount of game, large and small presented by Finn to the lady of the house as a token and a gift.

CHAPTER V.

NOD PAYS FINN A RETURN VISIT.

THE man Nod was tall and strong, well-shaped and erect, but of a grim and dour aspect, save only when his looks were turned upon his wife and child.   His cheeks were hollow and colourless, and though he was young his black hair already showed the blemish of early grayness.   He was proud, too, and the indignities which he had endured before the eyes of his wife and his people preyed upon his mind, so that his sleep forsook him and he wandered to and fro by night and by day like a dead man in motion. On the seventh day his wife brought to him a cunningly-prepared sleeping draught, and that night he slept well, yet on the morrow it was with great difficulty she persuaded him to set out on his journey to the Hill of Allen.   Yet he went and two

armed men with him. They crossed the
Slaney and the Barrow, rivers of Leinster,
and crossed the Plain of the Liffey, which
is now called the Curragh. Here they were
attacked by robbers, whom they defeated.
Nod behaved well in the conflict, for though
inexpert in arms he was by no means a
coward. On the tenth day, in the forenoon,
they saw the camp of the Fians on the Hill
of Allen—tents innumerable and banners
floating there with many devices. There
was one high above all the rest, which
showed the likeness of the golden sun half
risen from the blue floor of the sea. It was
the banner of Finn, and was a sign to all
men that Finn was there and that whoever
desired food and drink, or peace and happiness, or the redress of injuries, might come
to him, and all who were in any distress.

As Nod drew nigh to the camp he wondered more and more to see how carelessly
Finn and the Fians resided on this hill, for
there were no ramparts or moats or trenches
around the camp, and no towers of defence
or of observation; no strong palisades of
timber, therefore no gates. Also there were
no scouts or sentinels, and no bodies of
armed men, keeping the approaches to the

camp. The hill too, which was flat on the top, was no more than a great rising ground, and the broad green streets of the camp communicated with the open green plains of Kildare.

CHAPTER VI.

NOD MEETS SOME FAMOUS FIANS.

TREMBLING and sorely distressed in mind, Nod began to enter the camp. Before him was one very broad green street bordered on both sides by the white brown-roofed tents of the Fians, each tent standing apart by itself. All the people were of great stature, well shaped, and graceful in all their motions and brightly attired. There was a tall, very handsome young man standing by a tent upon the right side, which was the last there and touched the open country. The young man was talking pleasantly with two maidens who leaned from a window in an upper storey of that tent Yet he was not so much absorbed in the conversation as not to notice the coming of Nod and his company. He had long glossy and curling black hair, which rolled over a scarlet mantle. a round shield on his left arm and a spear in his right, his eyes were of bright hazel with long lashes, his complexion a rich brown, and smiles played ever sweetly round his red lips. Never had Nod beheld such an apparition of youth and beauty. He was tall too and straight and lissom as a young fir-tree which bends to every breath of the wind yet ever recovers its straightness.

The youth approached Nod, and when he had saluted him courteously and saluted also the man's servants one by one, he said—

" My lord Finn bade me meet thee and conduct thee through the camp to his tent. My own name is Diarmid."

As they went through the camp, Nod, who looked around him eagerly on every side, said—

" I see here on the left one strange tent standing by itself in a hollow. It is black, both sides and roof, and the banner over it is black with a pale device. There is a black man standing at the door, and two black hounds are beside him."

" Look no more," said Diarmid, " or it will be the worse for thee. I see him not, yet well I know that he is there. Few of us

ever see him.   His name is Dara-duff, from
the Black Mountain of the North."

Presently a company of young Fians met
them, descending the slope of the hill, and
laughing much as they came They enclosed
in their midst a man of great size, whose
head was bald.   He was fat, with a very big
stomach, and his eyes twinkled with
laughter and twinkled more as he drew
nigh, and took note of the stranger's
appearance.

He accosted Nod with mock politeness.

" Happy art thou," he said, " O illustrious stranger, for it is not necessary for
thee at any time to declare thy name and
breeding, for Nod is in thine eye and cut out
and carved all over thy countenance."

Diarmid's anger arose at this. He raised
the haft of his spear, and, as the fat man
turned to flee, brought it down with a
resounding noise upon the other's broad
back.   He uttered also a fierce rebuke.
Many of the Fians stood at the doors of their
tents watching this scene, and when they
saw the man beaten they laughed sweetly
and said—

" O Conan, thou wilt find a better sub-
ject for thy jibes and jests another time."

The fat man walked away crestfallen, and wiped a big tear from either eye. Now on the right sounded music and drums, trumps and trumpets of many kinds, so gay and exhilarating that Nod's sad heart leaped with animation as he heard it. Presently a battalion, emerging from the tents, crossed the green way swiftly, and disappeared on the left. They had a banner which showed the rowan-tree with green leaves and scarlet clusters of berries woven on a white ground. Then a troop of light-footed youths ran past them; beside each youth a hound bounded, led in leashes of white bronze or glistening silver.

Many bright or strange sights were seen by Nod that day, as he went with Diarmid through the mighty camp of the Fianna. Save the two already mentioned, there was no one who showed any blemish. All were of great size, well shaped and handsome, and every eye bright with the light of life. Through such sights and sounds Nod drew nigh to Finn.

CHAPTER VII.

FINN AT HOME.

THE door of Finn's tent was open, and so wide that an army might march through it. As Nod drew nigh trembling he heard low, very sweet music, like that of a recorder perfectly played, only sweeter. Then he saw within the tent a man of great size sitting upon a couch, whose hair was like snow and glittered like boiling silver poured out of the crucible. It was Finn. A young man whose name was Oscur sat beside him. He leaned his head upon Finn's shoulder and held Finn's left hand in his right. Behind Finn stood Dering, and upon the floor at Finn's feet sat another young man who whistled. It was his whistling that Nod mistook for the music of a recorder.

His name was MacLewy. It was one of Finn's chief pleasures listening to that young man as he whistled. Many of Finn's chief men were there standing or sitting through the great tent. There were daughters and granddaughters of Finn there too.

Finn saw Nod through the open door,
and started up and hastened towards him,
and he took him by the hand and led him
into the tent joyfully and affectionately, and
made him sit in his own seat. Finn's people
also, both men and women, welcomed him
with shining faces and pleasant words, and
they set before him a small beechen table
round and very white, and put before him
such viands as they had by them, also a
carved mether having four silver corners
and two silver handles, and Finn himself
poured out the ale. When Nod saw all this,
and how he, a man of no repute in Erin, or
of bad repute, nay the worst, was received
here with so much kindness, then the vein of
penury that was in Nod's heart brake. He
put his hands before his face and bowed his
head and wept aloud. When he had made
an end of weeping Finn put his hand gently
on his shoulder and said, ' I know it all, my
son. Eat and drink a little now, and afterwards one of my young men will lead thee
to the guest chamber. There thou shalt have
change of raiment and all else that thou
needest, and he will be thy companion till
the evening. Thou must sup with me here
this night and remain with me many days,

for thou hast suffered much, but now thou
shalt suffer no more.

CHAPTER VIII.

HOW MACLEWY CAME TO FINN.

BEFORE proceeding farther with Nod's
story, I desire to tell something about two
young men whom Nod found in the camp,
namely, the youth who was whistling for
Finn in his tent and the very handsome
youth who met Nod and conducted him
through the camp to Finn. And first concerning MacLewy, whose whistling was so
delightful to Finn.

Finn had a daughter named Lewy, and
Lewy had a son who, as he had no other
name, was called Lewy's son or MacLewy.
It was he who sat whistling before Finn
when Nod was approaching Finn's tent.
When this youth was born his mother con-
sidered with herself to whom she would
send him to be nursed. There was a celebrated nurse and instructor of children in
those days called Mongfinn or Fair-hair.
She had nursed and brought up in her time

eight hundred shield-armed warriors who were admitted into Finn's army. Lewy sent her child to her to be nursed and educated. When the boy was twelve years old the woman gave him a spear, sword, helmet, and shield, and sent him to Finn.

" Thou art a child," said Finn.

" I am a man," answered the boy. " Try me."

" Dost thou know the seven severe proofs to which I put candidates ?" said Finn.

" I know them," said the boy, " I did not come here to be engaged in conversation, but to be proved; and make your proofs stiff, for I promise you that they will be a laughing-stock when I have done with them."

At that Finn flushed and said, " Beware of pride and vainglory, my son; they soon come to a fall."

" Not where there is a corresponding or even excessive degree of merit to support them," answered the lad unabashed.

" Make me a poem according to the rules of the Imbus-for-Osna," said Finn, " every second line rhymed and every other line assonanced, and with three alliterations in every line. Let the theme be thy coming to Finn's house."

The boy made the poem on the spot, mag-
nifying himself and censuring the manner
of his reception. Also he glanced disparag-
ingly at certain of the great men who stood
around, Goll mac Morna, Ossian, and
others, mingling satire with his song.

"Thou art indeed an astonishing youth,"
said Finn.

" I thought I would astonish thee before
our interview came to an end," answered the
lad.

"Hold out thy spear," said Finn.
" Nay, lad, that will not do. Take it by the
extreme end, hold it at an equal distance
from the ground along its whole length, and
thyself perfectly upright the while."

The lad held the spear-end not in his
hand but with three fingers only. "Doth it
tremble ?" he said.

Unwillingly, and yet gladly too, they all
had to admit that it did not.

" That will do," said Finn; " I shall
put thee to no more proofs after that."

" That is to deprive me of my glory,"
said the boy; " I see that you are all jealous
of me already."

" Hast thou any amiable accomplishment ?" said Finn. "Canst thou play on an instrument ?"

"Set a battalion before me," answered the boy; "and me before it with my weapons of war in my hands, I will play upon it finely."

"I mean a musical instrument," said Finn, laughing.

"Yes," said he; "I play on an instrument."

"Is it with thee ?" said Finn.

"It is indeed," he replied, "now, and at all times. It is a flute, alive, red, flexible, with ivory keys white as May blossom."

"It is thy mouth," said Finn; "now play for us."

The youth whistled, and never before or since did such music pass the human lips. All who were in that presence wept save Finn only.

"Stop now," said Finn; "before my mighty men are dissolved away in salt rivers. Whose son art thou ?"

"I am the son of Lewy, and the grandson of Finn. Of my father I have no knowledge and no care."

"Thou art my man from this day forth," said Finn. The lad put his right hand into the right hand of his grandfather and became his man.

CHAPTER IX.

MACLEWY GETS INTO TROUBLE.

FROM the day that MacLewy came into the camp there was no peace in it, but all was disorder, confusion, noise, and quarrelling. There were the howling of dogs furiously chastised, and the noise of loud vauntings with fierce recriminations, and disturbances at ale feasts, and frequent rushings of Finn's champions through the camp to separate men engaged in deadly combat. It seemed as if the very genius of discord, confusion, and civil war were let loose in Finn's fraternal and affectionate host. One morning Dering awakened Finn and said, " There is some great thing forward to-day, O Finn. Come forth at once." Finn came to the door of his tent and there he saw the seven standing battalions of the Fians drawn up before him in marching array,

and over every battalion its own ensign, and
gloom, wrath, and mutiny in every face.
When Finn appeared the seven captains
stepped forward and stood before him, and
they said—

"Choose this day, O Finn, between thy
grandson and the army. If MacLewy re-
mains with thee, *we* go; if we remain with
thee the boy goes."

At that the army shouted approval, and
that shout went across the sea and was heard
in the court of Arthur, high King of the
Britons.

With difficulty Finn pacified the host on
that occasion. He promised them that he
would send away his grandson if within a
given time he could not tame his wild un-
tutored heart.

"Why is the host so enraged with thee?"
said Finn.

"It is because I am the best man
amongst them," said the lad; "and is it I,
thy grandson, who must instruct thee that
surpassing merit always provokes envy,
jealousy, and hatred?"

"Nay, nay, lad," said Finn; "Cuchulain,
son of Sualtam, was without dispute the
greatest hero in his time, and also the best

beloved. And remember what the historians record concerning him—

> He spake not a boasting word
> Nor vaunted he at all,
> Though marvellous were his deeds."

Finn took the lad to himself and trained and tutored him till he tamed his wild heart, and when his cure was complete he gave him back to the host, and after that none of Finn's men was more admired and loved than was MacLewy.

Finn's precepts which he used in the instruction of MacLewy were repeated to St. Patrick by Caelta, and St. Patrick bade his scribe write them in a book, and ordered his people to use them in the instruction of princes.

Here are some of them :—

> Pursue mildness, son of Lewy.
> Don't beat the hounds without good cause.
> Don't censure high chiefs.
> Keep two-thirds of thy politeness for women and humble people.
> Don't rage against the rabble.
> Strive to hold others in esteem and to like them ; so the host will not be offended though thou art loud and noisy.

Trust not in thy courage and thy great
strength, but consider well thy arms and thy
armour.   Then with confidence bend thy
knee to the battle, and thy brow to the pale
fierce fight, etc., etc.

CHAPTER X.

HOW DIARMID CAME TO FINN.

A SCORE of young warriors burst from the
wide doors of Mongfinn's house and ran joyfully across the lawn.   Their polished
shields leaped upon their backs as they ran.
It was May morning.   It had rained during
the night, but the sun now shone brightly
and the wet fields and trees glistened in his
rays.   The youths were Mongfinn's finished
scholars.   They came fresh from her hands,
each of them with her kiss and her blessing
on his head.   Whither did they run so
swiftly and with such joyful cries and exclamations ?   To the Hill of Allen, to Finn,
to be entered in the roll of his men, in case
they should pass the examination; and all
felt sure that they would pass.

Leaving the lawn they struck a narrow

path in the woods and ran on, one by one, making pleasant echoes in the still forest. When they emerged from the forest they came to a rocky ravine through which a torrent rushed. There were stepping-stones in the torrent, but they were now hidden, for the torrent was greatly swollen; a brown swirling mass of rough water rushed down the ravine.

Nothing daunted, the foremost of the party ran to the torrent, holding his two spears in front of him with the hafts forward, as boys now use leaping poles. He planted these on the edge of the torrent, and springing upwards, rose between them and propelled himself clear across the water. The rest did the same, only the youngest of the party fell back once, not having sprung with sufficient force, but encouraged by the rest he succeeded at the second attempt.

As they were proceeding on their journey they heard a groan, and, looking back, saw an aged woman leaning on a staff on the far side of the torrent, a little out of the way. She said, " You who are so young, strong, and happy, have pity on one who is old, weak, and sorrowful, for I cannot cross this wild torrent without aid."

" We cannot," they answered; " we are bound for the court of the most splendid captain on earth, and we must not appear in his presence in raiment soiled and dripping. Some strong churl will soon pass this way and take thee over the torrent."

So they went on their way, but not all. One of them, a tall and very beautiful stripling, stayed behind. His name was Diarmid. A second time he bounded lightly over the torrent, and having saluted the old woman respectfully, he raised her in his young strong arms and bore her through the ford. The torrent reached to his shoulders and was so violent that no ordinary man could have resisted it. Yet he reached the other side safely, and set her down carefully. As he was about to run forward again, he was aware of a tall, stately, and beautiful woman who stood by his side equipped like a warrior, her countenance so bright that it dazzled him to look upon it. Beside her stood a tall man, as glorious as the woman, but not armed. He smiled on the lad. " I know thee, O Angus," said the youth. " Wherefore hast thou played this trick upon me?" " To prove thy chivalry," he answered Then the man and the woman wrapped themselves in their magic mantle of woven air and were no more seen.

Diarmid pursued his party and came up with them as they were entering the camp.

When they came before Finn all the rest looked bright and clean and pleasant to the eye, but Diarmid's scarlet mantle, all but a little of it, was stained brown with the muddy water, and his white tunic with gold buttons was also defiled, and he looked like a spot in the midst of his comrades. When Finn saw him he said sternly, " Thou hast been wading in torrents to-day."

" I have," said Diarmid.

" Why did you not leap them like your comrades?" said Finn.

" That I cannot tell," answered the young man, with a blush.

Then Finn looked fixedly at him and said, " I can. I see thee crossing a swollen torrent with an aged woman in thy arms. And thou hast seen a glorious sight. It is still shining in thy face and in thy eyes. Thou shalt have success in war and success in love. All things good and nothing bad shall ever be told concerning thee at all time, and thy glory will last till the end of the world."

The woman whom Diarmid met at the
torrent was the war-goddess of the Gael :
the man was Angus Ogue, son of the Dagda,
the god of youth and beauty, from the fairy
Brugh on the Boyne.

> I lingered on the royal Brugh which stands
> By the dark-rolling waters of the Boyne
> Where Angus Ogue magnificently dwells.

CHAPTER XI.

NOD'S LIFE ON THE HILL.

BEFORE he came to Finn's camp Nod lived
alone in solitary grandeur in the midst of
inferiors. Now he lived amongst superiors,
which at first made him ashamed, but by
degrees his shame vanished and he began to
be happy. Soon he made dear friends and
comrades, and after that one day seemed to
him more joyful than another. He learned
the proper management of his weapons in
offence and defence. He delighted to watch
trials with hounds. He received as a gift
from one of his new friends a beautiful
hound, whom he called Son-of-the-Eagle.
He went to his first hunting shortly after
that, leading the dog with him. It was in a

forest belonging to Finn, in the country called Teffia. There Son-of-the-Eagle had the good fortune to hold a fine boar. Nod despatched the boar with a well-aimed thrust of his spear. His new comrades praised him and the dog warmly. It so chanced that while Nod was with Finn one of Finn's forests in the North of Ireland was disturbed by a lawless chief dwelling in the neighbourhood. Finn sent a troop to chastise him, and Nod was permitted to accompany the troop as a volunteer. Nod acquitted himself well in that expedition and was brought back to the Hill on a litter between four comrades, wounded but happy. He was indeed sore wounded, yet his recovery was rapid, so pure was his blood, and so light, gay, and alert his spirit. Nod could not believe that the world held so much happiness as seemed to fill the air upon the Hill of Allen. He went on two fishing expeditions to the Shannon, when he and his friends built for themselves booths by the river and had good sport, but wherever he went he was always glad to return to the camp on the hill. Cheerfully he arose in the morning and sweetly he slept at night.

CHAPTER XII.

NOD AND THE DRAGON.

WHILE Nod was on the Hill of Allen there came messengers from the west imploring Finn's assistance against a great water-dragon, which had newly come to the country, and had taken up his abode in Lough Derg, which is a great fresh-water sea formed by the river Shannon.

Such a dragon, they said, was never seen before in Ireland. He was more terrible, they said, than any of the numerous dragons which Finn had formerly slain.

Finn had killed dragons, monsters, apparitions, and savage beasts without number, and was enraged that another of that bad race should fear him and his men so little as to take up his abode in the midst of the island and lay waste the surrounding country.

This dragon killed and ate not cattle only, but men and women, and as he rolled through the country he destroyed forests and houses. He was of a blue colour, they said, and had a mane like a horse. Nearly every one who saw him died of fright.

Finn announced the news to his men, and they at once called upon him to lead them against the monster. All Finn's young men rejoiced greatly at this adventure, for the young men had never been at the killing of any serpent or monster, only they used to hear their seniors tell many tales concerning such adventures.

So they all went westward to the Shannon with great joy. When they reached Lough Derg the water of the lake was still and smooth. There was nothing to indicate that a terrible monster lay concealed in the depths. Some, more fanciful than the rest, declared that they saw a certain dark shadow, which they said showed the outlines of the beast's form at the bottom of the lake. Then they shouted all together and beat their swords against their shields in order to awaken the monster, and certainly if he could be awakened the noise they made was loud enough to rouse him. Presently there was an agitation in the water, which rose up like a mound in the midst of the lake, soon forming into waves and billows, and a dark-blue mass lifted itself out of the water.

It was the monster's head and neck : he had a mane like a horse. Then two eyes like two lamps showed themselves and glared at the Fians. The younger men, who were so anxious to hunt a dragon, now trembled and gradually moved away from the bank of the river. They were not expecting such a prodigy. When he saw the enemy the serpent raised his tail out of the water, and lashed the lake into storm in his fury, so that the spray fell all round the country for miles. Every Fian was as wet as if he had been dipped in the lake. Now the serpent roared with a voice like thunder, chilling the blood of the bravest of the Fians. His open red mouth was as wide as the gate of a city. This dragon was blue and had no wings or legs. He was in fact a monstrous serpent. He rolled on to the shore, and though many of the Fians gave back before him the majority did not. They surrounded him by the hundred, darting their spears against him, cutting at him with their swords, and though he rolled over and crushed them by the score, others supplied the places of those who fell. Finn from his place saw that the serpent was devouring

his men. With his great red tongue he
swept them into his mouth, using it as a
mower uses his scythe. No one behaved
more bravely than Nod, yet he was one of
those whom the serpent devoured. Above
the din of the battle Finn heard the lamentation and wailing of his men, as they disappeared in clusters down the serpent's red
throat.

"My dead will soon be more numerous
than my living," said Finn, and, so saying,
he sent Oscur against the reptile. If Oscur
could not kill him, no one else could save
perhaps Finn himself, and it was now a
great many years since Finn had engaged in
conflict with a beast of the kind. Oscur
stepped down valiantly to the serpent, and,
poising it, cast his spear at the beast's head.
The rush of Oscur's spear through the air
was like the raging of a hurricane through
a forest. But the beast was invulnerable.
Oscur's first spear and second spear sprang
back from the serpent's tough hide as a ball
springs back from a wall. When Finn saw
that, he called to him his son, Dara, who
was a very active and intrepid youth, and
he said to him, "Dara, I must go myself
against this monster. Watch me, and when

I say 'leap,' then lightly and valiantly
spring into the dragon's mouth, sword in
hand, and cut him open from the inside.
There only he is vulnerable." Oscur was
still engaged with the serpent, and though
he could not wound the serpent owing to the
thickness of the skin, he yet held him in
check. Finn, without sword, shield, or
spear, ran past Oscur and plunged his two
hands into the great hairy mane of the
beast.

As soon as he got a firm grip, using his
utmost strength, he raised the serpent into
the air and then threw him again upon the
ground, belly upwards. "Leap," cried
Finn. Dara forthwith sprang as he was, all
armed, and his sword in his hand, into the
serpent's mouth, and descended into his
terrible throat. There Dara, as soon as he
could secure a footing, and indeed that was
not easy, cut a slit in the serpent's throat,
and continuing cut it downwards for twenty
yards. Dara came out all red, but erect,
with his sword still in his hand, and
behind him in gory heaps rolled out
all the warriors whom the serpent had
swallowed. The serpent was partly
choked by Finn, and partly killed by

Dara's sword.   Dara won great honour by this adventure.   This was looked upon as one of the bravest leaps ever made in Ireland, and it must be confessed that it is not everyone who would spring into the throat of a dragon.   Dara was called Dara the Red after that, viz. Dara Derg.   Dara did many other brave feats in his time, but this was regarded as his masterpiece.   A river of blood rolled from the serpent into the lake, and after this the lake was called Lough Derg, *i.e.* the Red Lake.

Nod, as you may imagine, was not ready to engage in other adventures for some time after this.   When taken from the gory heaps that rolled from the serpent, and when he was washed, it was found that there was no hair on his head, and his broken armour was crushed everywhere into his mangled body.

A couch of healing was a second time made for Nod, and Finn's surgeons and his beautiful nursing-women attended him, and Finn himself, with pleasant words, came every day to his bedside.   Yet, in spite of his sufferings, no sooner was Nod healed than he clamoured to be led against the only hydra known to exist in Ireland.   It was a

black female serpent called Ethnea, which
dwelt in a gloomy tarn then called from her
Lough Ethnea, but which is now called
Glendalough. Such a torrent of warlike
ardour and love of adventure now flowed
perpetually from Nod's heart.

Finn would not attack that serpent because it was foretold to him that her
destruction was reserved for a holy druid of
the coming time, whose name would be
Caemhghen (*i.e.* Beautiful Born) or, as
we pronounce the word, Kevin. That
serpent is supposed to have been the death-
goddess of the Gael. The holy youth Saint
Kevin, Christ's servant, destroyed her in the
power of Almighty God, maker of all
worlds.

CHAPTER XIII.

THE LAST OF NOD.

IT was evening in Nod's valley and the sun
was descending. The summer was over, and
the autumn and winter were in the air.
Nod's wife was in her house, guiding and

directing her people, who were making the winter store of candles. One of the out-door thralls ran in and said—

"O lady, there is a brilliant company of young heroes coming to the house."

"They shall be welcome," said Nod's wife. "What kind of man is the leader of the band?"

"He is young," answered the other, "tall, and very handsome, with abundant hair as black as the raven, and his complexion clear, so that the blood shows like scarlet in his cheek. He is gay and cheerful, talks and laughs much, and with his spear points out distant places to his companions. There are a score of young men with him, all of a noble appearance, also a company of little boys riding on horses."

"That young man is my husband and your lord," said Nod's wife to her people, but they answered firmly that he was not.

Then she threw round her shoulders her best mantle and clasped it in front with a shining brooch, and, followed by her personal attendants, went out to meet the company, leading her little son by the hand.

The young man was indeed Nod, but so altered that no one in the palace, save his

wife only, recognised him.   All the early
grayness had gone from his hair, and his
cheeks were full and rosy and his eyes
bright, so that one could hardly desire to see
a happier, or handsomer, or more attractive
young man than was Nod after his six
months' visit to Finn and his stay amongst
the Fians.   Finn used to billet his men upon
the country during the winter, and Nod
undertook to entertain, that winter, as
many men as he would be permitted to take
with him.   The boys riding on horses were
the sons of divers of his new friends.   They
were to be his foster-children, to be brought
up in his house along with his own son.   Very
joyful was the meeting between husband
and wife on that occasion.

Here, then, we will take leave of Nod and
his wife.   I have only further to add that
Nod became as famous for hospitality as he
had been formerly notorious for the want of
it.   So greatly was he changed that he was
said to be the third most hospitable man of
his time in all Ireland.

Let me add that Nod was not so much a
penurious man as penury itself and dark,
fierce selfishness, and the story shows how
Finn by force, example, and precept, taught

the men of Ireland to live in a more generous, kindly, and humane manner than they had done. Those who look deeper into these strange stories will find that the numerous serpents which Finn slew were ugly practices and savage unnatural habits.   Finn, like the Greek Apollo and the Greek Hercules, was famous as a serpent-slayer.

The following story will not be pleasing to those who think that the famous King Arthur could do nothing wrong.   It is pleasant, however, to find that two such illustrious men as Finn and Arthur, though they had their quarrel, finally became good friends

CHAPTER XIV.

FINN AND KING ARTHUR.

ONE day Finn hunted his forest of Ben Edar; that was the old name of the Hill of Howth, near Dublin. The game of this forest were wild oxen. Only the best dogs were brought out that day, for the urus was

an animal of great size, strength, and
ferocity. Finn invited Arthur, King of the
Britons, to share in that hunt. Arthur
came in his galley with twenty-seven men,
and took up his station at the head of the
harbour, in order to turn back the wild oxen
should they take to the water when hard
pressed by the hounds. Finn sat on a rock
called the Cairn of Fergal, midway between
the top of the hill and the sea, rejoicing in
the music of the crying hounds, the roaring
of the oxen, and the shouting of his men.

Three dogs chanced to pursue a great ox
along the shore of the harbour and dragged
him down close to where Arthur stood.

" There are not in the world hounds like
these," said his men to Arthur, " and let us
now put them on board our galley and sail
away before the Fians break through the
woods and come to us."

Arthur consented. They put the dogs
on board the galley, hoisted sail, and, grasp-
ing their oars, lashed the blue sea into foam.
Presently there was nothing visible of
Arthur and his people save a faint white
track on the distant horizon. The dogs were
Bran, and the Leopard, and a third called
Adnuaill. When they put to shore in

Briton-land they went straight to the mountain of Lodan, the son of Lear, and hunted that forest with great joy and signal success. No one, not even Finn, seated though he was upon the cairn, saw the taking of the dogs.

In the evening, after Finn had divided the spoil, the dogs were counted, as was customary with them, and their tale was three short. Finn called out the names, and Bran, the Leopard, and Adnuaill were missing. There was great sorrow amongst the Fians at the loss of their three matchless hounds which were the glory of the western world, and many of the men wept. Then Finn called for pure water, and when he had washed his hands he put his thumb to his divining tooth, and it was revealed to him that Arthur had taken away the hounds to Briton-land and was hunting the mountain of Lodan, the son of Lear.

Finn selected nine men to go in pursuit of the hounds, with Goll mac Morna for their captain, and Oscur, son of Ossian, to crush every enemy in their path. The nine went to the top of the Hill, in the gray dawn of the day, and looked across the sea to Mananan's Island and " fasted upon him,"

that he should send them his magic boat.
They were not long there, when they saw the
boat coming. It had no sails and no oars.
There was not a man on board, yet the boat
leaped and sprang from wave to wave,
glittering with gold and pearl. She came
to the harbour of Ben Edar, and the nine
men got on board, and again the bark beat
out into the open sea conducting the heroes
to Briton-land. They disembarked and
marched to the mountain of Lodan and
searched the forest through, till they came
to the great booth which Arthur and his men
had made for themselves. Arthur and his
men were at supper when Finn's people
entered the booth.

Arthur welcomed them and bade them
sit down to supper.

" We are come for Finn's dogs," said
Goll mac Morna. " If we are to have them
peaceably we will accept your hospitality.
If not, look to your arms, for we will not
leave this house without bringing our dogs
with us."

" Then you will not leave this house at
all," said Arthur. " For I give you my
word, that I would rather see all Finn's men
rolled in bloody shrouds than surrender

these dogs.   And as you are bent upon war,
war you shall have."

Then weapons screeched and flashed,
and a terrible and murderous battle ensued,
and the end of the fighting was, that all
Arthur's men were slain, and he himself
was wounded.   Finn's men were closing in
upon him to slay him, when Oscur son of
Ossian sprang forward, and throwing one
arm round Arthur, stood against the eight,
though their battle-fury was on them, and
that was no small proof of Oscur's in-
trepidity and no small proof of his warlike
prowess, when the eight gave back and let
him have his way.

They buried the dead honourably, and
set up their mounds and pillar stones, and
returned as they came, bringing the three
hounds and Arthur.   Ere they left the
palace, Goll spied in one corner of it a
great gray steed, and in another a beautiful
bay mare.   He took them with him as
plunder.   There were no horses like them
in the world.

When they brought Arthur before Finn,
Finn asked him why he had done that deed,
and Arthur bade him look at the hounds
and he would cease to be surprised.   He

also added, " O Finn, thou hast thy compensation already for that wrong, for I have lost many dear comrades, and my two matchless steeds; keep them, and let the quarrel between us end here."

Finn was satisfied with that proposal, and Arthur remained with him till he was healed, and when he departed Finn dismissed him with kind words, rich and numerous gifts, and a guard of honour. All the horses that were in Erin after that descended from the two steeds which Goll mac Morna took out of Arthur's house in the mountain of Lodan the son of Lear.

Finn and his men, however, only used horses for racing. They were themselves infantry, and went always on foot. Yet they were fond of horses and had them in great numbers. The following is a verse in one of Caelta's poems which he recited for St. Patrick :—

Three rivers, that used to pour from Finn's camp
On a May-day morning when the sun shone brightly,
A river of men and a river of horses and a river of
    hounds.

PART III
FINN AND THE HISTORIAN

CHAPTER I.

THE HISTORIAN HAS A WELCOME VISITOR.

AT the end of a day's hunting Finn and Dering found themselves alone with their two dogs. When Finn wound his horn there was no answering horn. They then went forward, looking around on every side for some sign of human habitation. At last they saw a light and went towards it. The light came from a large shining lamp set in the gate-tower of a handsome dwelling-place. There was a moat, and inside the moat a wall, and within the wall a good-sized house with trees around it. The drawbridge which spanned the moat was drawn up, but on the side of the moat on which the two men stood was an iron gong, and beneath it a stout club. Dering seized the club and beat upon the gong.

The people of this fort had already retired to rest, but the master was awake. He was sitting beside his fire, arranging a number of beechen tablets on which many things seemed to have been written in strange letters. In fact the man was reading, for in those days books were made of timber. The beechen tablet which he held in his hand contained the history of Finn and his men. He had written this history himself, and was getting the tablets into better order, and lamenting that there were so many things in Finn's history with which he was not acquainted. At the other side of the fire was a boy very sleepy and nodding.

Said the man, " Oh, that Finn might lose his way some night when he is hunting, and come here for rest and refreshment. He would tell me the things I want to know. Then I could fill up these empty tablets. Boy," he said, " have not the Fianna been hunting all day in the next forest?"

" Truly, O master," said the boy; " I myself ran from height to height watching them, but the chase passed away southwestward."

The man groaned. Just then both man and boy started from their seats, for they heard the thunderous roar of the great iron gong struck by the hand of Finn's man.

" Run, boy," said the man of the house;

" see who is at the gate and bring me word."

The boy ran, climbed into the gate tower, and swiftly returned.

" My lord," he said, " there are without two men of great stature. The elder and taller of the two is the most beautiful being that these eyes ever saw. His hair is pure white and rolls in masses over the scarlet mantle that surrounds his mighty shoulders; his complexion is fresh and ruddy, and his eyes are blue. There is beside him a hound which he leads by a chain of silver attached to a collar of gold. That hound is a wonder. She has a small head, eyes as terrible as a dragon, and a white spot on her black breast. The man's companion is brown-haired, and he leads by a bronze chain a spotted leopard."

" Put wings to thy feet, lad," cried the old man in great excitement; " raise the portcullis and let fall the bridge, for the men are Finn and his man Dering, and thy leopard is only Bran's spotted sister. Haste! haste!"

Meantime Dering would have once more thundered upon the gong, but Finn restrained him.

The old man joyfully received these
welcome guests. As all his people had been
awakened by the thunder which Dering had
roused from the gong, an excellent supper
was soon got ready for the two Fians. Bran
and the Leopard had their supper that
night served to them in a silver dish, a vessel
of great price, for it was the proudest and
happiest night in that old man's long life,
and well he knew that not Finn only, but
those two dogs, would be famous while
night and day endure. When they had had
their supper Bran and the Leopard came
and lay down upon the hearth before the
fire, and the old man scanned them closely
with great awe and reverence. Bran's ears
were red, her legs yellow, the rest of her
body was black, save for a round white spot
on her breast, and a starry shower of white
over her loins. The Leopard was spotted
yellow throughout on a ground of black, the
spots growing smaller and more frequent
towards the neck, and very small upon the
head and ears. Of the two, the Leopard
seemed to be the more powerful, and Bran
the swifter and more spirited. Both dogs
were sleek and glossy. There was no beast
in the world which they would not overtake

and pull down. The Leopard's real name
was Sgeolan.

CHAPTER II.

FINN'S HUMBLE RELATIONS.

" I LIKE thee well, old man, for many
things," said Finn, who had now ended his
supper. " Thou hast entertained us nobly
and like a king, without officiousness or too
hospitable zeal, and hast suffered us to eat
our supper in peace, which hungry men like
best. I perceive, too, that thou art a lover
of dogs like myself, and that there flows
from thee a strong torrent of affection and
admiration for my two matchless hounds;
and if a man loves my dogs, he shall ever be
dear to me. I perceive, also, that thou art
a historian, and historians are very dear to
me."

The old man answered, " O captain of
the Fianna, thy dogs are famous over the
whole world, and will be famous to the
world's end; nor am I surprised at their
glory when I look upon them, and this is the

first time I have seen them near at hand.
Often have I inquired concerning their birth
and breeding, but no man could relate it.
The wisest of them said it is unknown."

"It is unknown," said Finn.

"I would give much to learn," said the
old man.

"Many have expressed the same wish,'
answered Finn.

The old man set drinking vessels on a
small table near the fire, also a great
measure of ale, and when the two guests
had washed their hands in ewers of water,
and dried them in napkins, they drew nigh
to the fire. Finn blessed the man and his
house, and took a deep draught, draining
the last drop from the huge tankard, while
the old man wondered.

Finn looked earnestly at him and said—
"Bid the servants go to bed, and I will tell
thee. I will tell thee other things, too, and
thou shalt fill thy empty prepared staves."

The old man obeyed joyfully, and when
he had shut and bolted the doors of the
chamber, he returned. He thought his heart
would break with excess of joy. Then he
sat down at the one side of the fire, and, for
the first time, looked at Finn towering on

the other, his mighty limbs and huge
knotted knees, and his countenance like the
sun.

" Long ago," said Finn, " for no man
who now lives remembers these things,
when first my passion for hounds came upon
me, I was in my booth on the slopes of the
Slieve Bloom Mountains. It was night,
and I in my bed. Without a storm raged,
and the roar of the forest surrounded me,
with thunder and lightning and the rush-
ing of rain. I lay awake rejoicing in the
uproar; but while I listened I heard amid
the noise a very small and delicate sound,
like the tinkling of some exquisitely modu-
lated tympan, exceeding sweet. I must tell
thee, too, that ere this my mother's sister
was lost and could nowhere be found, and it
was supposed that she had been spirited
away by the Fomorian enchanters, and was
seen subsequently in the form of a beautiful
hound. I heard a knocking at the door of
the booth, and when I opened it, I was at
first dazzled with the flood of light which
came in through the door. I thought it was
very near lightning   Then I perceived a
woman standing there, tall, and wondrous
beautiful. with a closed basket in her hand.

She gave me the basket, and said—' I have brought these to thee, O Finn, for I have always heard that cousins should be cousinly.' I saw no more of the woman, and when I drew back into the booth and had stirred up the embers and made a blaze, I opened the basket and discovered there two blind puppies of exactly the same colour as those which lie before thee on the hearth. They have been with me ever since," said Finn, " and they are with me now. These hounds, then, matchless for beauty, speed, courage, strength, and intelligence, are my own cousins," said Finn.

CHAPTER III.

FINN TELLS ABOUT HIS CHILDHOOD.

" WIN victories and blessings for ever, O captain of the Fians of Fail," answered the old man. " That, indeed, is a strange and memorable story, nor am I surprised at it when I contemplate their beautiful proportions, and think of their rare intelligence and sagacity, of which I have heard many

things. And now, O Finn, if it would not
be irksome to thee, I would gladly learn
somewhat of thy boyish life. As long as I
can remember thou hast been famous and
powerful, ruling in the midst of thy unconquerable warriors and indefatigable hunters. But men tell vaguely of a time, long
ago, when thou wert solitary and surrounded
with peril of many kinds. They also say
that the sons of Morna searched the world
for thee, to slay thee, when thou wert a
young child. But of these things they
speak vaguely. If it would not weary thee,
I would gladly learn these things with more
exactness from thy own eloquent and cor-
rectly-speaking lips."

" I will tell thee somewhat," said Finn.
" It will not weary me, for I am by nature
eloquent, and speech flows from me without
effort. I was a babe in the cradle when that
great battle was fought in which my father
was slain. The conquerors, viz. the sons of
Morna, forthwith spread themselves over
Ireland with the object of exterminating
all my father's sons and grandsons, and, in
fact, our whole race. A fierce company
came straight from the battle to my
mother's house to kill me. No news of

the battle had yet reached my mother, when two strange women entered the house, snatched me from the cradle before her eyes, and fled. They were leaving the palace by one door when my enemies were entering by the other. The latter gave chase, but they might as well have chased the wind as chased those women. The women brought me to the depths of the forests which clothe the Slieve Bloom Mountains. There I was weaned, and dwelt as a child with the two women in the forest, cowering low before the wrath of the sons of Morna, whose trackers and searchers continued seeking for me. That was how I survived the slaughter of all my father's house."

CHAPTER IV.

FINN'S FIRST QUARRY.

" I WOULD know now, O Finn," said the old man, " what game, bird or beast, first fell by thy hand. Now indeed thou art a mighty hunter, thy forests are everywhere, and thy game laws embrace all Erin. Few are the houses in which a hound-whelp is not being reared for thee, and, truly, the great game and the small which fall before thee in any one year, who could number? But of all fame there is a beginning, as the mightiest river has a small source."

"That is true," said Finn, "and I will tell thee. Afterwards my protectors fled with me out of the Slieve Bloom Mountains, for the sons of Morna discovered my retreat, and they put a ring of men and dogs round the mountains, and were closing inwards. Nevertheless, the heroines bore me safely through them all, and fled with me into the extreme west of Munster, beyond the beautiful glen which is called Glengariffe, to a place on the haven of Bera, which is known as Dunboy. There they built a hut on the edge of a wood close to a small lake. I used to play on the shore of the lake, and send smooth finger stones skimming along the surface, and soon began to shoot very straight and far. One day a wild duck came sailing past with her brood of twelve ducklings. I took a good aim at her with a carefully-selected stone. She saw the missile approaching, leaping from

point to point on the smooth water, and
with her wings began to beat the water in
the act of raising herself for flight. Yet the
stone struck her and cut off her two wings.
The bird, accompanied by her orphaned
brood, drifted towards the shore, and when
I could reach her, I seized her joyfully, and
also took and put in my bosom the twelve
ducklings, and so hastened to the house,
where the heroines praised me much for my
skill and success. The plucking, the roast-
ing, basting, and carving of that duck gave
these persons and myself as much pleasure
as was ever got out of any similar adventure. That," said Finn, "was my first
exploit as a hunter."

CHAPTER V.

FINN AND THE POETS.

" It is reported," said the old man, " that
no one understands or loves poetry better
than thyself, and I know that no youth can
be enrolled amongst thy Fians unless he can
make a good poem."

" I myself made that law," said Finn,
" for many good reasons, and chiefly for
this, that youths who love poetry are more
readily inflamed to the performance of great
deeds, are more obedient to their captains,
and hold their banner and their battalion in
greater esteem. One rude bone-hewer may
indeed conquer a youth of the kind I love,
but set against each other two armies, one
of warlike boors and the other such as are
my Fians, and they are not to be compared.

" My own poetic nature I inherit from
my mother. It was she who composed that
lullaby which begins, " Sleep, my child, in
soft slumber sleep." She came secretly to
the place where the heroines guarded me,
and took me in her arms and to her bosom
and sang that lullaby and departed.

" After the first hunting exploit which
I have described, I hunted perpetually, and
got food for my protectors. Then the
passion of poetry grew upon me. There
were six poets who lived together in a dell
in the Galtee Mountains I abandoned my
protectors and went to live with them, and
they taught me I lived with these sons of
wisdom and beauty till one day when a
robber and plunderer out of Leinster came

and slew them all and took me away captive and compelled me to live with him in his den, which, like a stork's nest, was in the midst of a cold, bleak, desolate marsh, a wide watery expanse of sorrow.

" Afterwards, when I was a young man, I came to the beautiful Boyne, hearing that the wisest men were there. I became servant to a man who called himself Finn; my own name then was Demna. It chanced that the day I entered his service he had taken a salmon in the pool of the Boyne which is called Linn Féc. He bade me bake the salmon and serve it. When I set the salmon before him, he asked me whether I had tasted the fish. I said, ' no,' but that I had touched it with my thumb to know if it were sufficiently baked, and afterwards put my burned thumb into my mouth. ' Alas,' he said, ' the prophecy is fulfilled. This fish is not for me, but for thee. It is the Salmon of Knowledge, and thou art the true Finn, about whom the prophets have been prophesying from ancient days. Sit in my place and eat the fish.' So I sat in his place and ate the Salmon of Knowledge. That is the reason why, when I put my thumb under my divining tooth, the know-

ledge of things past and to come is revealed
to me.

"I remained on the banks of the Boyne
with the wise men there till I had mastered
all the mysteries of poetry and all the knowledge which it contained in that art. On
the day that I was initiated and admitted
a member of their learned company, I composed a poem in proof of my poetic skill."

"Prithee repeat it for me," said the old
man.

Finn repeated it.

"May-day! delightful time! how beautiful the
    colour,
The blackbirds sing their full lay.
  Oh that Laeg were here.
The cuckoos sing in constant strains.
  How welcome the noble
Brilliance of the season ever. On the margin of
    the branchy woods
The summer swallows skim the streams.
  The horses seek the pool.
The heath spreads out its long hair.
  The weak white bog-down grows.
Sudden consternation attacks the signs. The planets
    in their course running exert an influence.
The sea is lulled to rest, flowers cover the earth."

Finn repeated the poem slowly in order

that the old man might remember it. The metre was complicated and intricate, and the poem throughout riveted with many shining alliterations, so that it might be the more easily remembered, and defy the assaults of time.

CHAPTER VI.

FINN REVEALS HIMSELF FURTHER.

" It is on account of my poetic nature and my close intimacy with many excellent poets that I have pleasures which are not usually enjoyed by warriors and hunters. Dear to me is the cry of sea-gulls and the thunder of the great billows of the Atlantic against the cliffs of Erris, the washing of water against the sides of ships. and the sound, foam, and motion behind them as they cleave the fluid sea, for not dearer to me is the firm earth than the never-resting ocean.   I love to hear the clear flute of the blackbird in the morning, and the thrush's song as he sits by himself and sings when the sun goes down.   The beautiful changes of the varying year are sweet to me, and truly there are not many sights and sounds that I do not love, or from which I do not derive pleasure, so that solitude is no more irksome to me than company, and yet I am the most sociable of men; so that I do not surround myself with guards and royal state, but live simply in the midst of my people, like one of themselves, for I love them well, and well they love me."

The old man, still thirsting for knowledge, said, "O Finn, tell me who is the best man, and who is the worst among the Fians."

Finn answered, " I myself am the best man, and Dara-duff from the Black Mountain is the worst. There is a great deal of life in me," said Finn; "and a great deal of life goes out of me. There is death in him, and a great deal of death goes out of him. Yet he never had less power than he has now. Even if I could destroy him, I am not permitted to do so, for his roots spring mysteriously out of the roots of the world. He has been in the world always, and will be in it till the end of time."

"Dismiss me now to my rest and my slumber, O amiable and much-inquiring

historian !" said Finn; " for I arose early
this morning, and that was an early rising
when a man could not see the sky between
his outspread fingers, or distinguish the
leaves of the oak from those of the beech."

While this conversation lasted Dering
had shown no signs of sleep or drowsiness;
he sat erect, listening with bright eyes.

In the morning Finn asked the historian
many questions concerning his manner of
work, and commended him, and gave him
good counsel, as, for example, " that he
should not, in making his histories, concern
himself exclusively with wars and things
horrible, but should tell also of the common
daily life of men and women; let women
and children," he said, " be frequent in
your stories, for they are the light of life,
nor let the sun be long absent from your tale,
seeing that he himself is never long absent
from us. Also," he said, " I perceive there
is some domestic sorrow in thy mind. What
is it ?"

The old man said that he had a very dear
grandson who was sick of a decline.

" Bring him to me," said Finn.

Finn looked upon the lad and asked
whether there was a well of pure water in

the neighbourhood, and when they answered him " Yes," he bade them lead him to it.

There he scooped up the sparkling water in the hollow of his right hand, and when he had spoken some poetry in a strange tongue, he gave to the young man to drink.   From that day the youth steadily recovered.

Finn caused the whole household to come before him.   He spake kind words to them all, and he blessed the old man and his people, and went away with Dering and the dogs, and they saw him no more.

PART IV

THE COMING OF FINN

CHAPTER I.

NOBLE ANCIENTS IN ADVERSITY.

Now that you are sufficiently acquainted with Finn as he appeared in the fulness of his power and glory, I desire to let you see him in his youth, while he was struggling upwards out of obscurity, when he was friendless, solitary, and surrounded by enemies. The lesson taught by Finn in his power is the lesson of flowing goodwill towards men. From his youth we learn the lesson of cheerfulness and courage.

In the heart of Connaught, a deep track-less forest, and in the heart of the forest a rude booth of timber, rudely roofed with rushes and heather. Brushwood grew above it and around it, so that one might pass many times and almost touch the house without discovering it. In this booth, one wild December evening, half a dozen old men—very old men—sat crouched around a small fire of sticks. They were clad in ancient rags, and in skins; their faces were thin and hunger-bitten; their fingers long,

lean, and crooked. The meanest of them
looked a king. Fate had pressed very hard
on these old men, but had not conquered
them, and their eyes shone under most rigid
brows. Who were these noble old men clad
in rags and skins, nourishing here in
poverty and famine some unconquerable
resolution? I shall tell you.

The captain of the Fians in his time was
Cool, son of Trenmor, the mightiest of the
Fian captains down to his time, and Cool,
remember, was the father of Finn. Then
the sons of Morna revolted against him,
saying that Goll mac Morna, their brother,
was the better man and should be captain. Each party drew together an army,
and the battle for the Fian leadership
was fought on the banks of the Liffey.
There Cool was defeated and slain; the
sons of Morna triumphed and raised their
brother Goll to the leadership. Luchat
Mael was the champion who slew Cool and
took from him his satchel, which contained
the jewels of sovereignty and right leadership. He slung it to his own girdle. While
he kept that bag, the tyranny of the sons of
Morna was secure, and it was supposed that
there was not a champion in the world who

could conquer Luchat Mael.   What these
jewels were is not rightly known, but there
was great power and virtue in them.

After the battle, the sons of Morna went
through Ireland exterminating all the
breed and seed of the overthrown family.
Nearly all the warriors of Cool who escaped
from the battle were obliged to make terms
with the new tyranny, and swear allegiance
to Goll mac Morna.   A very few did not.
These were the old men whom we saw, clad
in rags and skins, crouching around their
feeble fire in the booth in the forest.

At first they lived by hunting, poaching
it might be called, for all the forests and all
the game belonged now to Goll mac Morna.
They shifted from mountain to mountain
and forest to forest, from lake to river and
river to lake, for the trackers and searchers
of the sons of Morna were on their traces.
Finally they were pressed into greater
confinement, so that they could only hunt by
night and by stealth, and while one man
speared a salmon, there was another who
kept watch, and oftentimes they were
acquainted with the soreness of famine.
Yet even thus they refused to make terms
with the new tyranny.   " To the sons of

Morna," they said, " we will oppose a resolution which hunger and death shall never
break."   But hardship and years began to
tell upon their iron frames, and their great
limbs wasted away. Then some of them
grew too old to do anything but sit by the
fire and keep it alive, while those who were
not so old set traps and springes near the
cabin, and sometimes snared a few birds
and small game, and sometimes did not.
Often the very old warriors turned hungry
eyes on the others as they came back empty-
handed, but no word of reproach was ever
uttered, nor at any time one word signify-
ing that famine had expelled their heroic
determination from their hearts.

This night the younger men returned,
bringing with them a red-winged thrush.
Silently they plucked the bird and sus-
pended it over the red embers by a twine
of twisted grass. Grimly the seniors smiled
as the small bird revolved over the glowing
embers and dropped its scant fatness, which
hissed slightly as it met the fire. They
thought of nights in the Speckled House on
Hill of Allen long ago, the feasts there, the
strong carousing, and all the joyous and
glorious days and nights of their youth,

when Cool, son of Trenmor, their captain, was strong and unsubdued.

"Brothers, we are coming very near the end," said one noble elder. "There is little nourishment in this thrush, and yesterday and the day before we had not even a thrush. Be it so, but I would like to die hearing that the tyranny of the sons of Morna was shaken."

"Dear friend, that thou shalt both hear and see," answered the one relative of Cool who had escaped the fury of the Clanna Morna and the hosts of their trackers. His name was Crimall, son of Trenmor; he was chief over them. "It was surely foretold to me, how, by a friendless and solitary youth, a banned, outlawed child of the wilderness, the sovereignty of the sons of Morna would be overthrown."

"That we believe," they said, "for it was surely prophesied, but not that the youth in skins would arise in our time."

The bird being now roasted, Crimall made an even division of the same, viz. a seventh part to each man. Then he said, "O my coevals, listen to me. I now tell you tidings which I have concealed for a dark hour like this. The youth of many prophecies has

appeared and there is perplexity in the
councils of Goll mac Morna. He and his
fierce warriors are already looking for the
end."

In spite of sore famine the old men
dropped their morsels and gazed upon the
withered senior. "Yes, dear and faithful
brothers," continued Crimall, " he has appeared; now from one point, now from
another, he descends upon them out of the
wilderness to burn and to slay, and again
the wilderness covers him. He has the
strength of a hundred men; he is swifter
than a deer, terrible as a dragon, and
glorious as the sun on his fiery wheels. So
much I know for a certainty; the end truly
draweth nigh. We, the few and faithful,
will again sit at the right hand of our own
Fian-captain, in the flashing hall of the
Tech Brac, on the flat-topped hill."

"Oh, that we could believe thy words,
Crimall, strong-hearted and wise, but even
while we speak, the trackers of the Clanna
Morna may be at the door, and the youngest
of us has not the strength even to raise the
heavy swords, which were like switches in
our hands while our power and manly force
were still with us."

"Hark," said one of them, "even now
I hear some man bursting through the
brushwood and young trees. Stand to your
weapons, my brothers; it is an enemy, for
friends in all broad Erin we have none."

CHAPTER II.

THE OLD MEN HAVE A STRANGE GUEST.

It was pitiful to see the response to this
challenge, for, though all stood up and
sought to arm themselves and stand on their
defence, they were not able. With difficulty they raised their mighty shields, and
their huge swords trembled in their ancient
and nerveless hands.

Someone knocked at the door, and, as it
seemed, with the butt-end of a great spear,
the weak door was splintered with the blow.
The strongest and youngest of the Fians
stood behind the door and cried, "Art thou
a friend or an enemy?"

"A friend," answered a young, cheery,
and laughing voice from without.

" Unbar the door," cried old Crimall.
" Deceit is not an attribute of the Clanna
Morna—I will do them that justice. There
was no lying or treachery found amongst
them at any time. Unbar the door."

" There is mockery in the voice," said
the old Fian. " It is the voice of one who
laughs."

" Nay, not mockery," answered Crimall,
" but laughter only. It is the laughter of
a young and happy heart. Unbar the
door."

The old Fian unbarred the door, and a
young man, large and mighty-thewed,
entered the booth laughing, his whole face
suffused with sparkling tides of some great
joy. He was white and ruddy, his bright
face lit up the whole gloomy chamber of
age and sorrow. His lips and cheeks were
smooth, the golden masses of his hair rolled
over his wide shoulders. He wore a huge
rough mantle of many skins of wild-boars
sewn together; his shirt was of deer-skin
laced with leathern thongs; his knees bare,
and his moccasins of untanned hairy ox-
hide. He carried a great shield and spear;
the bright end of a scabbard projected below
his black skin-cloak. He came straight to

Crimall and bending low in reverence
said—

"Noble elder, I am a hunter lost in
these woods. I seek supper and a bed, for
I am homeless and supperless."

"Thou art right welcome, O youth,"
said Crimall. "We too are hunters, but
fortune has not smiled on our labours this
day. Nevertheless what we have with us in
the booth is thine."

A sylvan seat, which, indeed, was only
the sawn end of a tree, was set before the
fire for the young hero, and while he conversed with Crimall, the others contributed
their small fragments. Then a platter con-
taining the just dismembered bird was
given to him.

"Would we had better to offer thee, O
illustrious youth whom the gods love, but
we can give thee pure water from the spring
and a pleasant bed of heather and rushes,
and our young men will rise early in
the morning and search the snares and
springes. Haply some birds or animals
may be taken therein on which thou mayest
break thy fast well. Music we cannot give
thee, for music hath not been heard amongst
us for a long time; but there is one amongst

us who is a good historian, and will entertain thee with stories of old times till sweet
sleep makes heavy thine eyelids."

The laughing light died out of the
young man's eyes and lips, as the glittering
sunshine glancing on a million waves fades
from the sea when a black cloud comes over
the sun. He looked at the wretched repast
upon the beechen platter, the little fragments in number the same as the number
of the old men. He marked their hollow
gray faces and their eyes bright with
famine, bright too just then with the light
of kindness and goodwill. He laid the
platter on the ground beside him, and put
his great hands before his face, and bowed
down his head and wept. The old men
preserved silence. Youth, they thought,
hath many sorrows which cold age cannot
comprehend.

CHAPTER III.

THE GUEST PROVES HIMSELF AN EXPERT HUNTER.

WHEN the boy had made an end of weeping, he stood up and said—

" Noble old men, good fortune in hunting doth not fall to every one each day, but sometimes one man meets with it, and sometimes another. Ill fortune was yours to-day and may be mine to-morrow, but this day success has attended my hunting, and there is with me a sufficiency of food for all. Put on the fire, I pray you, fresh timber, not little sticks but big logs, and make a good fire, for we shall all feast well to-night."

So saying he left the booth, while the old men, wondering, gazed at one another, and he presently reappeared bending in the low doorway and bearing a deer on his shoulders, the two fore legs caught in one hand on his breast, and the two hind legs in another, while the head, with lolling tongue and branching antlers, hung down on one side. It was no fallow-deer, but a great red-deer of the forest, a buck, very large and fat. Out over his head then he flung the huge carcass, which fell with a heavy dull sound and a clash of the clattering antlers on the floor of the booth, and went out, and returned carrying in his right hand a tusked boar held by the bristling hair, and in his left a sow grasped by a leg, and flung them down beside the deer. He returned once more trailing behind him a long string of small game, hares and badgers, wild geese and swans, fastened together by a stout cord of cut and twisted hide, so that all the farther end of the booth was heaped with birds and beasts.

"Truly thou art a mighty hunter, O brave and generous youth," said Crimall, "but bring in now thy hounds. Why shouldst thou leave them without? We too, alas! love hounds, and thine will be most welcome at our hearth."

"Truly there are no hounds with me," said the lad. "Whatever be the powers that fashioned me, they have made my limbs swift and tireless, so that even the red-deer are not apt to escape from me when I get

upon their traces. Yet, why should I boast?
You, too, have doubtless in your day run
down swift game. Verily, the tongue of youth
is apt to be loud in declaring its own glory.
Here I think is a sufficiency of meat, and
I chance to have bread too, for I am not a
hunter only, but a warrior and spoiler; I
sacked a lime-white noble Dûn this day,
and have brought with me some of the
spoil."

CHAPTER IV.

FINN.

" HAST thou any other surprises in store
for us, O youth, beloved of the gods?" said
Crimall, who trembled as he spoke, for fear
and hope made him like ice and fire.

" What thing above all other things in
the world wouldst thou see with greatest
joy, son of Trenmor, son of Basna?"

And Crimall answered straight—

" The bag that was at my brother's
girdle in the battle of Cnoca, with his
jewels of sovereignty and power within it,

and the head of Luchat Mael, and both in
the hands of my brother's only son."

"I have them with me," cried the lad,
as he threw back his boar-skin mantle, and
held out the jewel-bag in one hand and a
huge black head in the other. "Here is
Cool's treasure-bag and the treasures in it,
and here is Luchat Mael's head, whom I met
and slew this day in fair fight, and I am
Cool's youngest son whom the druidesses
bore away after the battle, and I am waging
war on the Clanna Morna and rending their
tyranny, and all Ireland is a shaking sod
under my feet."

Then the old men all together cried aloud
for joy, yea, they screamed together like
eagles or the sea-gulls of the cliffs of Erris
when they wheel and cry in their multi-
tudes between the gray cliffs and the sea, so
the old men cried; and they flung their
arms around the youth and kissed his head
and his cheeks, and his shoulders, his hands,
and feet, and wept till their voices were
choked with lamentation, and their eyes
became like rivers of salt water, and a third
part of the night went by before they made
an end.

Afterwards they washed their faces in

pure water, and laughed as much as before
they wept.   Then they turned their minds
to supper, and skinned and cut up the game,
and roasted great steaks of venison on the
red embers.   Also they cleared out the old
disused Fian oven, and stewed and seethed
great quantities of flesh in steam, and if
they had any bright attire left, or any orna-
ment, it was brought forth, and they ate,
and drank, and caroused, and related to
each other their many adventures, and the
old men ever kept their eyes upon Finn and
noted every word that came from his mouth.

When they had conversed for a long time,
Finn said : " Now, if it is pleasing to you,
I will play for you on my *clairseach* and
sing, for what is a feast without music and
singing ?"   From his great boarskin mantle
then he produced a little harp and removed
the sheath of fine soft white doeskin, and,
when he had turned the pegs and brought
the strings to the correct tone, he said : " I
will sing you my own songs, that you
may judge of my proficiency in poetry, as I
learned it from the six poets with whom I
associated in the woody dells of Slieve
Crot."   He sang for them a song in praise
of the wind, beginning —

Sweet to me is the voice of the wind,
Alike when he whispers in the leaves
And when he sounds his strong *dord* in the tree-
tops,
Bending the forests in his wrath.

He sang a second song in praise of the sea, " the boundless unconquerable realms of Lir," and a third in honour of the sun, and a fourth in honour of the earth.

Crimall said, " Those are good songs, my son. I like thy verses well and especially those in honour of the firm, strong, rocky, and all-supporting earth. We, the Fians of thy sire, were accustomed to kiss the earth three times before we went into any battle."

" That custom shall be maintained," said Finn; and then he said, " I have a wonder with me, that is to say, a man and a woman, and they are not seen. The man's height is the span of my hand, and the woman's somewhat less, and there are not in the seen worlds, or in the unseen, a pair of singers and musicians like them. Cnu-Derole and Blana, sing and play for the noble Fians, who were my father's dear friends and comrades."

Thereat the Fians heard slow, sweet, fairy music and singing, strange, unearthly harmonies and songs in an unknown tongue, low, faint, and remote. The Fians wept hearing them.

"They are husband and wife," said Finn; "and they never cease to be in love with each other. They are with me always, and I am as dear to them as they are to me."

"You have another wonder at your girdle," said Crimall, "though you know it not. I mean the inexhaustible horn that is in thy father's treasure-bag. Wash thy hands, my son, and be not afraid to remove it. It is wrapped in the skin of an ermine." Finn washed his hands, and took out the horn, and removed the ermine skin. The horn was rimmed with silver and had little breastplates of crystal, like eyes. "Fill the horn," said Crimall, "and hand it to me." Finn did so, and Crimall took a long, deep draught out of it, and handed it to the old man who sat next him, who did the same, and handed it to a third. So it came to Finn last, who thought that he surely would empty the horn; but when he gave over, the horn was not half empty, and when he put it again in Crimall's hands it was full to the

brim and overflowing. Crimall took the
goblet and emptied it into the fire. There
went up from the fire a thick blue smoke,
shot with stars and lightnings, and a sweet
perfume filled the whole booth.

" That is indeed a wonder," said Finn;
" this goblet must be one of the marvels of
the earth."

" It is," said Crimall; " the name of it is
Elba.   I shall tell thee its story another
time.   I have shown thee its properties now
to teach thee the nature of the treasures
contained in that bag, in order that you may
cherish and safeguard it.   That horn has
other properties also.   If it is filled with
water, he who drinks will find in it the
liquor that he likes best, and this will
happen whether the horn be filled with
fresh water from the spring or with salt
water from the sea.   That bag is filled with
instruments of enchantment."   Finn carefully wrapped up the goblet and put it back
into the bag.

Finn, of course, told the old men all his
history.   The following is his account of the
way in which he won his wife.

CHAPTER V.

FINN'S LOVE STORY.

" AFTER I escaped from the watery strong-
hold of that robber who had slain my friends
and tutors, the six poets, I was with the two
heroines once more in the Slieve Bloom
forests. I used to hunt for them continually,
and our larder was never empty. When I
next went abroad, I came to Bantry, on the
shore of the great bay of Bera in the south.
I offered my services to the King of Bantry.
He asked me what I could do, and I said I
could hunt. The King of Bantry made me
his hunter. I used to hunt for him in the
woods and mountains of the wild adjoining
country. There was one spot there very
dear to me on account of its beauty; it is
called the Rough Glen (Glen-gariffe). There
are beautiful little bays and inlets of the sea
there, and overhanging mountains and
streams, and delightful woods. The birds
sing there in the winter. Once while I was
hunting at a distance from home, I saw a

number of people assembled, kings, and
nobles, and noble ladies in holiday attire—
a very gay and delightful scene. I came to
the assembly and mingled with the wild
people of the district who were onlookers.
No one knew me in that place, nor was it
known anywhere, save to my two benefact-
resses, that I was the lost son of Cool, son of
Trenmor. Amongst the noble ladies was
one seated on a throne, with others in at-
tendance on her, and guards. She was
young, but looked proud and disdainful.
Never before in dreams or with my waking
eyes had I seen any maiden so beautiful. I
turned to a bystander and said, " Who is
this princess who is like the morning star,
and what is the meaning of this assembly?"
She heard me, for there was a waiting
silence upon the assembly, and turned her
eyes towards me.   Then she started, as I
thought, and blushed and looked away
quickly.

" The bystander answered, ' Thou art
surely a stranger in this country. That
princess, who is like the morning star for
beauty, is the only daughter of the King of
Rushy Ciarraí. Many noble youths and
famous champions have sought her in mar-

riage, but from the first she declared that it
was a *ges* to her' (a druidic commandment)
' not to marry any man who could not leap
yonder deep cleft in the mountain side; and
truly it is an awful leap, and those who have
attempted it are at the bottom of the cleft.
There has been no relenting in her, and no
compassion, so powerful is the *ges*, as some
think, or so great is her love of virginity,
as others say. This morning a king's son
named Crimthann hath promised to leap
the chasm or perish there like others.'

" I pressed through the wild people, and
knew that she was ever aware of my doings
even when pride restrained her from looking towards me. I was clad in my skins,
and these fastened together in any wise. I
came to the nobles, and saluting them
respectfully, asked whether I might pass
through that presence and examine the
cleft. For answer two of them undertook
to push me back, but I stood like a rock
against them, and they and others at the
same time raised against me their voices
and their weapons. The maiden was
agitated and alarmed at this, and said,
"Let the hunter youth examine the cleft if
it be pleasing to him. See you not that he

is a stranger?" All in my skins as I was, truly a wild spectacle, I bowed low to the maiden, and thanked her for her courtesy, and went to the chasm's edge. Far below, a torrent ran through the ravine, so distant that it was dumb; and at the other side were sharp crags and crooked points of rock. I measured the distance with my eye, and felt certain that I could make the leap, for, owing to my manner of life, I was truly a good leaper. I returned, and, because I had found favour in her eyes, came and took my stand amongst the nobles and men of war, and was well received by them on this second occasion.

"Then from the west there came a splendid company, led by a young man nobly attired, wearing a brooch of gold in his five-times-folded mantle; a very graceful youth, whose form and shapely limbs seemed to promise success in that venture, so that the blood seemed to stand still in my heart, for fear that he might succeed, and when I looked to the maid she was pale, too, fearing that the young man might accomplish the leap.

"He approached, and having made her a reverence, and addressed her and her

people in an eloquent manner, he withdrew,
and stripped off his mantle and jerkin of
fine satin, so that there was upon him only
a close-fitting light shirt. He took off his
shoes, too, and put on others carefully prepared for such a feat. Then, when he was
in readiness, a trumpet sounded, and he ran
towards the chasm, having the fleetness of
a deer and the gracefulness of a fawn, so
that I said, ' Surely the man will leap the
cleft and I shall die.' But when he neared
the chasm and saw the crooked rocks and
crags at the other side, and became aware
of the dark, fearsome depths of the ravine,
he hesitated and swerved, baulking the leap.
Then the maiden looked at me, and from her
two eyes, and her lips, and her whole countenance, I saw love for myself pour forth in
torrents, and she saw the same flow from me
to her, for no one observed us on that
occasion.

" The young man, Crimthann, after he
had been encouraged by his people, addressed himself to the leap a second time,
and yet a third, but he ever swerved, baulking the leap; and in the end broke into tears
and went away. Then I arose, and, taking
courage, stood before the throne and offered

to take the leap which Crimthann had refused, if the maid would accept me for her husband. She was silent and pale with terror, and did not answer. Her father and the attendant nobles told me that she would not, and, laughing, they bade me save my neck for the service of my king, and that whole bones were better than broken ones, and other such-like speeches.

" I said that I would not take an answer from them, only from the damsel, that it was her and not any of themselves I desired to marry. She said somewhat in a low voice to her father. He raised his head and said, laughing—

" ' She says that she never saw anyone worse dressed.'

" That may be," I answered, " but it is not my skins that I propose as a husband, but myself, and my question is not answered."

" After a further colloquy her father spoke again and said—

" ' My daughter is sorry to have taunted thee with thy attire, and she could wish her husband in other things to resemble thee, but will not consent to the leap.'

" Then," said I, " if the damsel will not

give me the same promise that she made to
others, I shall leap the chasm notwithstand-
ing, and having reached the far side I shall
return to my lord."

"When she heard that, and saw that I
was fully determined, she burst into tears
and consented, and her father said—

"'I am truly sorry for thee, O brave
youth, and how shall I make an excuse to
thy lord, who is my foster-brother, when he
learns that between us we have killed his
man?'

"Then rejoicing, I chose my distance
from the chasm's edge, and I threw off none
of my attire, only laced it with a thong close
to me that the skins might not impede me
in my flight over the cleft. And I ran to the
edge and sprang, though a woman's scream
rang in my ears, and rose with an airy bird-
like motion, and lighted with my two feet
on the other side on smooth ground beyond
the rocks, and in like manner I sprang
back, and I approached the noble company
and asked them whether that was sufficient,
speaking deliberately, for I was in no way
exhausted or out of breath. They were
astonished and pale, but when I offered to
do it again they said that it was enough.

" In this manner I won my dear wife.

" I went with that company to the King of Rushy Ciarraí's palace, and I got there splendid raiment fit for a king's son, and our marriage was celebrated with great honour. And now, dear friends, I tell you one of my secrets. There is a prophetic faculty with my wife, and the vision of unseen things. It was revealed to her that my death would come swift and bloody in any year in which I might neglect to take that leap both backwards and forwards on the first day of May, from the East to the West at the rising of the sun, and from the West to the East at his setting."

When Finn lay down and slept that night the old men conversed with each other joyfully in low tones, but indeed that precaution was not necessary, for Finn's sleep could not be disturbed or broken by the voices of friends.

CHAPTER VI.

THERE WAS FEAR IN TARA.

IT was the Eve of Samhain, which we Christians call All Hallows' Eve. From of old it was a night on which many strange things used to happen. In fact it was a great festival with our pagan ancestors.

The King of Ireland sat at supper in his palace at Tara. All his chiefs and mighty men were with him. This king was called Conn, and surnamed the Hundred-Fighter. He was a celebrated king, very big and strong, red-haired and blue-eyed. On his right hand was his only son, Art the Solitary, so called because he had no brothers. The sons of Morna, who kept the boy Finn out of his rights and were at the time trying to kill him if they could, were there too. Chief amongst them was Goll mac Morna, a huge and strong warrior, and captain of all the Fians ever since that battle in which Finn's father had been killed. There is a heroic story told about this Goll which shows that he was as brave

as he was strong.   Once he was about to
engage in a great battle, and his generals
pointed out to him that by making a night
attack upon the enemy's camp, an easy
victory might be won.   Goll answered :
"When as a boy I first took arms of chivalry
and was presented with my weapons, I
swore that I would never attack an enemy
by night, or use against him any stratagem
or unfair advantage.   That promise I have
kept down to the present time; I will not
break it now, and I will not break it while
I live."

You may remember that when Finn
knocked at the door of the booth in which
the old Fians were assembled, and called
himself their " friend," Crimall ordered
the door to be opened, for he knew that
neither Goll nor any of his people could use
the deceit of calling himself a friend in
order to gain an unfair advantage. In fact,
none of the Fians at any time were ever
accused of telling a lie.   " We, the Fians,
never lied," sang Ossian; " falsehood was
never attributed to us."

Goll and his mightiest men were there
that night. The great long table was spread
for supper.   A thousand wax candles shed

their light through the chamber, and caused
the vessels of gold, silver and bronze to shine.
Yet, though it was a great feast, none of
these warriors seemed to care about eating
or drinking; every face was sad, and there
was little conversation, and no music. It
seemed as if they were expecting some
calamity. Conn's sceptre, which was a
plain staff of silver, lay beside him on the
table, and there was a canopy of bright
bronze over his head. Goll mac Morna,
captain of the Fians, sat at the other end of
the long table. Every warrior wore a bright
banqueting mantle of silk or satin, scarlet
or crimson, blue, green, or purple, fastened
on the breast either with a great brooch or
with a pin of gold or silver. Yet though
their raiment was bright and gay, and
though all the usual instruments of festivity
were there, and a thousand tall candles shed
their light over the scene, no one looked
happy.

Then was heard a low sound like thunder,
and the earth seemed to tremble, and after
that they distinctly heard a footfall like the
slow, deliberate tread of a giant. These
footfalls sent a chill into every heart, and
every face, gloomy before, was now pale.

The king leaned past his son Art the
Solitary, and said to a certain druid who
sat beside Art, " Is this the son of Midna
come before his time ?"   " It is not," said
the druid, " but it is the man who is to conquer Midna.   One is coming to Tara this
night before whose glory all other glory
shall wax dim."

Shortly after that they heard the voices
of the doorkeepers raised in contention, as
if they would repel from the hall someone
who wished to enter, then a slight scuffle,
and after that a strange figure entered the
chamber.   He was dressed in the skins of
wild beasts, and wore over his shoulders a
huge thick cloak of wild boars' skins,
fastened on the breast with a white tusk of
the same animal.   He wore a shield and two
spears.   Though of huge stature his face
was that of a boy, smooth on the cheeks and
lips.   It was white and ruddy, and very
handsome.   His hair was like refined gold.
A light seemed to go out from him, before
which the candles burned dim. It was Finn.

CHAPTER VII.

FINN SECURES A PROMISE WITH GUARANTEES.

HE stood in the doorway and cried out in a strong and sonorous but musical voice :

"O Conn the Hundred-Fighter, son of Felimy, the righteous son of Tuathal the legitimate, O King of the Kings of Erin, a wronged and disinherited youth, possessing nowhere one rood of his patrimony, a wanderer and an outlaw, a hunter of the wildernesses and mountains, claims hospitality of thee, illustrious prince, on the eve of the great festival of Samhain."

"Thou art welcome whoever thou art," answered the King, "and doubly welcome because thou art unfortunate. I think, such is thy face and form, that thou art the son of some mighty king on whom disaster has fallen undeserved. The high gods of Erin grant thee speedy restoration, and strong vengeance of thy many wrongs. Sit

here, O noble youth, between me and my only
son, Art, heir to my kingdom."

An attendant took his weapons from the
youth and hung them on the wall with the
rest, and Finn sat down between the King
of Ireland and his only son.   Choice food
was set before him which he ate, and old ale
which he drank.   From the moment he
entered no one thought of anything but of
him.   When Finn had made an end of eating and drinking he said to the King—

" O illustrious prince, though it is not
right for a guest to seem even to observe
aught that may be awry, or not as it should
be in the hall of his entertainer, yet the
sorrow of a kindly host is a sorrow too to his
guest, and sometimes unawares the man of
the house finds succour and help in the
stranger.   There is sorrow in this chamber
of festivity.   If anyone who is dear to thee
and thy people happens to be dead, I can do
nothing.   But I say it, and it is not a vain
boast, that even if a person is at the point of
death, I can restore him to life and health,
for there are marvellous powers of life-
giving in my two hands."

Conn the Hundred-Fighter answered,
" Our grief is not such as you suppose, and

why should I not tell a cause of shame,
which is known far and wide? This, then,
is the reason of our being together, and of
the gloom which is over us. There is a
mighty enchanter whose dwelling is in the
haunted mountains of Slieve Gullion in the
North. His name is Allen, son of Midna,
and his enmity to me is as great as his
power. Once every year, at this season, it
is his pleasure to burn Tara. Descending
out of his wizard haunts, he standeth over
against the city and shoots balls of fire out
of his mouth against it till it is consumed.
Then he goes away mocking and trium-
phant. This annual building of Tara, only
to be annually consumed, is a shame to me,
and till this enchanter declared war against
me, I have lived without reproach."

" But," said Finn, " how is it that thy
young warriors, valiant and swift, do not
repel him, or kill him?"

" Alas!" said Conn, " all our valour is
in vain against this man. Our hosts en
compass Tara on all sides, keeping watch
and ward when the fatal night comes. Then
the son of Midna plays on his druidic instruments of music, on his magic pipe and
his magic lyre, and as the fairy music falls

on our ears, our eyelids grow heavy, and
soon all subside upon the grass in deep
slumber.   So comes this man against the
city and shoots his fire-balls against it, and
utterly consumes it.   Nine years he has
burnt Tara in that manner, and this is the
tenth.   At midnight to-night he will come
and do the same.   Last year (though it was
a shame to me that I, who am the high king
over all Ireland, should not be able myself
to defend Tara) I summoned Goll mac
Morna and all the Fians to my assistance.
They came, but the pipe and lyre of the son
of Midna prevailed over them too, so that
Tara was burned as at other times.   Nor
have we any reason to believe that the son
of Midna will not burn the city again to-
night, as he did last year.   All the women
and children have been sent out of Tara this
day.   We are only men of war here, waiting
for the time.   That, O noble youth, is why
we are sad.   The ‘ Pillars of Tara ’ are
broken and the might of the Fians is as
nought before the power of this man.”

“ What shall be my reward if I kill this
man and save Tara ?” asked Finn.

“ Thy inheritance,” answered the King,
“ be it great or small, and whether it lies in

Ireland or beyond Ireland; and for securi-
ties I give you my son Art and Goll mac
Morna and the chiefs of the Fians."

Goll and the captains of the Fianna
consented to that arrangement, though
reluctantly, for their minds misgave them
as to who the great youth might be.

CHAPTER VIII.

FINN TRIUMPHS.

AFTER that all arose and armed themselves
and ringed Tara round with horse and foot,
and thrice Conn the Hundred-Fighter
raised his awful regal voice, enjoining
vigilance upon his people, and thrice Goll
mac Morna did the same, addressing the
Fians, and after that they filled their ears
with wax and wool, and kept a stern and
fierce watch, and many of them thrust the
points of their swords into their flesh.

Now Finn was alone in the banqueting
chamber after the rest had gone out, and he
washed his face and his hands in pure

water, and he took from the bag that was at
his girdle the instruments of divination
and magic, which had been his father's, and
what use he made of them is not known, but
ere long a man stood before him, holding a
spear in one hand and a blue mantle in the
other. There were twenty nails of gold of
Arabia in the spear. The nails glittered
like stars, and twinkled with live light as
stars do in a frosty night, and the blade of
it quivered like a tongue of white fire. From
haft to blade-point that spear was alive.
There were voices in it too, and the war-
tunes of the enchanted races of Erin, whom
they called the Tuatha De Danann,
sounded from it. The mantle too, twinkled
in the blue, and the likeness of clouds
passed through it. The man gave these
things to Finn, and when he had instructed
him in their use he was not seen.

Then Finn arose and armed himself,
and took the magic spear and mantle and
went out. There was a ring of flame round
Tara that night, for the Fians and the
warriors of Conn had torches in their
hands, and all the royal buildings of Tara
showed clear in the light, and also the dark
serpentine course of the Boyne, which

flowed past Tara on the north; and there,
standing silent and alert, were the innumerable warriors of all Erin, with spear and
shield, keeping watch and ward against the
son of Midna, also the Four Pillars of Tara
in four dense divisions around the high
king, even Conn the Hundred-Fighter.

Finn stood with his back to the palace,
which was called the House-of-the-going-
round-of-Mead, between the palace and
Conn, and he grasped the magic spear
strongly with one hand, and the mantle
with the other.

As midnight drew nigh, he heard far
away in the north, out of the mountains of
Slieve Gullion, a fairy tune played, soft,
low, and slow, as if on a silver flute; and
at the same time the roar of Conn the
Hundred-Fighter, and the voice of Goll like
thunder, and the responsive shouts of the
captains, and the clamour of the host, for
the host shouted all together, and clashed
their swords against their shields in fierce
defiance, when in spite of all obstructions
the fairy music of the enchanter began to
steal into their souls. That shout was heard
all over Ireland, echoing from sea to sea,
and the hollow building of Tara reverber-

ated to the uproar. Yet through it all could
be heard the low, slow, delicious music that
came from Slieve Gullion. Finn put the
point of the spear to his forehead. It
burned him like fire, yet his stout heart did
not fail. Then the roar of the host slowly
faded away as in a dream, though the captains were still shouting, and two-thirds of
the torches fell to the ground. And now
succeeding the flute music, sounded the
music of a stringed instrument exceedingly
sweet. Finn pressed the cruel spear-head
closer to his forehead, and saw every torch
fall, save one which wavered as if held by
a drunken man, and beneath it a giant
figure that reeled and tottered, and strove
in vain to keep its feet. It was Conn the
Hundred-Fighter. As he fell there was a
roar as of many waters; it was the ocean
mourning for the high king's fall. Finn
passed through the fallen men and stood
alone on the dark hill-side. He heard the
feet of the enchanter splashing through the
Boyne, and saw his huge form ascending
the slopes of Tara. When the enchanter
saw that all was silent and dark there he
laughed, and from his mouth blew a red
fire-ball at the Tech-Midcuarta, which he

was accustomed first to set in flames. Finn
caught the fire-ball in the magic mantle.
The enchanter blew a second and a third,
and Finn caught them both. The man
saw that his power over Tara was at
an end, and that his magic arts had
been defeated. On the third occasion
he saw Finn's face, and recognised his
conqueror. He turned to flee, and though
slow was his coming, swifter than the
wind was his going, that he might recover
the protection of his enchanted palace
before the "fair-faced youth clad in
skins" should overtake him. Finn let fall
the mantle as he had been instructed, and
pursued him, but in vain. Soon he perceived that he could not possibly overtake
the swift enchanter. Then he was aware
that the magic spear struggled in his hand
like a hound in the leash, "Go then if thou
wilt," he said, and, poising, cast the spear
from him. It shot through the dark night
hissing and screaming. There was a track
of fire behind it. Finn followed and on the
threshold of the enchanted palace he found
the body of Midna. He was quite dead,
with the blood pouring through a wound in
the middle of his back, but the spear was

gone.   Finn drew his sword and cut off the
enchanter's head and returned with it to
Tara.   When he came to the spot where he
had dropped the mantle, it was not seen,
but smoke and flame issued there from a
hole in the ground.   That hole was twenty
feet deep in the earth, and at the bottom of
it there was a fire always from that night,
and it was never extinguished.   It was
called the fire of the son of Midna   It was
in a depression on the north side of the hill
of Tara, called the Glen of the Mantle,
Glen-an-Bhrait.

Finn, bearing the head, passed through
the sleepers into the palace and spiked the
head on his own spear, and drove the spear-
end into the ground at Conn's end of the
great hall.   Then the sickness and faint-
ness of death came upon Finn, also a great
horror and despair overshadowed him, so
that he was about to give himself up for
utterly lost.   Yet he recalled one of his
marvellous attributes, and approaching a
silver vessel, into which pure water ever
flowed and which was always full, he made
a cup with his two hands, and, lifting it to
his mouth, drank, and the blood began to
circulate in his veins, and strength returned

to his limbs, and the cheerful hue of rosy
health to his cheeks.

Having rested himself sufficiently he
went forth and shouted to the sleeping host,
and called the captains by their names,
beginning with Conn. They awoke and
rose up, though dazed and stupid, for it
was difficult for any man, no matter how he
had stopped his ears, to avoid hearing Finn
when he sent forth his voice of power. They
were astonished to find that Tara was still
standing, for though the night was dark,
the palaces and temples, all of hewn timber,
were brilliantly coloured, and of many hues,
for in those days men delighted in splendid
colours. When the captains came together
Finn said, " I have slain Midna." " Where
is his head ?" they asked, not that they dis-
believed him, but because the heads of men
slain in battle were always brought away
for trophies. " Come and see," answered
Finn. Conn and his only son and Goll mac
Morna followed the young hero into the
Tech-Midcuarta where the spear-long
waxen candles were still burning, and when
they saw the head of Midna impaled there
at the end of the hall, the head of the man
whom they believed to be immortal and not

to be wounded or conquered, they were filled
with great joy, and praised their deliverer
and paid him many compliments.

" Who art thou, O brave youth?" said
Conn.   " Surely thou art the son of some
great king or champion, for heroic feats
like thine are not performed by the sons of
inconsiderable and unknown men."

Then Finn flung back his cloak of wild
boars' skins, and, holding his father's
treasure-bag in his hand before them all,
cried in a loud voice—

" I am Finn, the son of Cool, the son of
Trenmor, the son of Basna, I am he, whom
the sons of Morna have been seeking to
destroy from the time that I was born; and
here to-night, O king of the kings of Erin,
I claim the fulfilment of thy promise, and
the restoration of my inheritance, which is
the Fian leadership of Fáil."   Thereupon
Goll mac Morna put his right hand into
Finn's, and became his man.   Then his
brothers and his sons, and the sons of his
brothers did so in succession, and after that
all the chief men of the Fians did the same,
and that night Finn was solemnly and
surely installed in the Fian leadership of
Erin, and put in possession of all the woods

and forests, and waste places, and all the
hills, and mountains, and promontories,
and all the streams and rivers of Erin, and
the harbours and estuaries, and the harbour dues of the merchants, and all ships,
and boats, and galleys with their mariners,
and all that pertained of old time to the
Fian leadership of Fáil.

NOTES

Arthur, a mythical King of Britain, chief of the Knights of the Round Table. See Tennyson's *Morte d'Arthur*.

Bru-fhear, a farmer, a husbandman.

Caelta = Caoilte Mac Ronain (pr. *Kweelta Mac Ronawn*).

Cláirseach (pr. *Clawrshach*), a harp.

Cnoca (Irish *Cnucha*, now Castleknock, near Dublin) battle of, fought in the reign of Conn the Hundred-Fighter. The contending parties were, on the one side, Conn the King, aided by the Fianna of Connacht; on the other side, Cool, the father of Finn, with the Fianna of Leinster, aided by Owen More, with a large army of Munstermen. The Leinster and Munster forces were defeated. Goll slew Cool with his own hand.

Crimhthann (pr. *Crivhann*).

Danann Maiden, Niamh (pr. *Niav*) of the golden hair, with whom Oisin went to Tirnanoge.

Diarmuid O'Duibhne, the Achilles of the Gael, the noblest character among the Fianna.

Dord, a humming; bass in music.

Eocha Moymheodhoin (pr. *Eochy Moyvyóne*), King of Ireland, died A.D. 365.

"Fasted upon him." This fasting process was an old custom of the Irish, and was regarded with superstitious awe. "He who does not grant a request to fasting is an evader of all."

147

Gabhra (pr. *Gowra*). Battle fought A.D. 284 at Garristown, Co. Dublin, between the King of Ireland aided by the Clanna Morna on the one side and the Southern Fianna on the other. The Southerners were defeated. Oscur and the King were slain.

Imbos-for-osna, a mystical rite used when making a certain kind of verse. The rite was called " *Imbos* " from " *bos*," the palm of the hand. " Palm-knowledge of enlightening."

Laeghaire (pr. *Laerya*), King of Ireland at the coming of St. Patrick.

Mether (Irish *Meadar*), a drinking-cup.

Ossian, Oisin (pr. *Usheen*), son of Finn. He was the chief Filé or poet of the Fianna.

Rushy Ciarraí (*Ciarraidhe Luachra*), a district in Kerry.

Samhain (pr. *Sou-in*), All Hallows' Eve.

Slieve Crot (the mountain of harps), now Mount Grud in barony of Clanwilliam, Co. Tipperary.

Slieve Gullion, in Co. Armagh.

Talkend (Irish *Táilcheann*), adze-head, a name given to St. Patrick. The meaning is doubtful. The *Seanchus Mór* says the Táilcheann is the party to whom all persons will humble their heads in genuflexion.

Tech brac (Irish *Teach breac*), speckled house.

Teffia, an ancient territory partly in Westmeath, partly in Longford.

Urus, a kind of wild ox.